She'd forgotten what it was like to make love with her husband.

He was sleeping now, his head pillowed on her chest. She rested her hand on his head, her fingers threaded through the silky-soft hair, and thought about the past year.

All the times they'd tried to make a baby, that was all they'd been able to think about. This time, not thinking about a baby, or failure, or if it was just the right time, they'd been able to concentrate on each other.

It had been wonderful. When he'd turned up, she thought it was going to be a disaster, and true, her plans had gone well awry, but there was no way she could call what had happened between them a disaster.

It was going to make it all the harder, though, when he left....

Will they...?

Won't they...?

Can they...?

The possibility of parenthood: for some couples it's a seemingly impossible dream. For others, it's an unexpected surprise.... Or perhaps it's a planned pregnancy that brings a husband and wife closer together...or turns their marriage upside down?

One thing is for sure, life will never be the same when they find themselves having a baby...maybe!

This emotionally compelling miniseries from Harlequin Romance® will warm your heart and bring a tear to your eye....

Look out for:
The Pregnancy Plan (#3714)
by Grace Green
on-sale August 2002

THE BABY QUESTION

Caroline Anderson

TORONTO • NEW YORK • LONDON
AMSTERDAM • PARIS • SYDNEY • HAMBURG
STOCKHOLM • ATHENS • TOKYO • MILAN • MADRID
PRAGUE • WARSAW • BUDAPEST • AUCKLAND

ISBN 0-373-03697-3

THE BABY QUESTION

First North American Publication 2002.

This edition published by arrangement with Harlequin Books S.A.

Visit us at www.eHarlequin.com

Printed in U.S.A.

PROLOGUE

LAURIE felt the first twinges of failure with dismay.

Not again, she thought despairingly. We can't have failed again. *I* can't have failed again.

An hour later she was curled up on the sofa with the dog at her side, a low, gnawing ache eating at her, waiting for the phone to ring, for Rob to ask how she was.

Meaning *that,* of course.

Oh, well, she'd get through it. She always did. Month after month she braved his disappointment—and the same old arguments. He'd had a test, which proved he was fine. Why didn't she have a test? At least then they'd know what they were dealing with, and there was so much they could do these days. Why not give it a try?

Because she didn't want to know it was her fault. She didn't want to go down the route of IVF and all that palaver. She was only twenty-six, and they hadn't been trying *that* long. There was plenty of time.

Wasn't there?

But she couldn't spend it like this. She couldn't spend yet another month waiting with bated breath for failure to strike.

There must be something else she could do with her life. Something more productive, less soul-destroying than sitting around being serviced fruitlessly like a barren cow.

She scrubbed the tears from her cheeks with the back

of an angry hand, and stood up, unravelling her long legs and wandering through to the study with the dog at her heels. She'd look on the Internet. Maybe that would offer some suggestions—and, if not, fiddling on the computer would at least pass the time.

She found a website address that looked interesting, and clicked on it, but it was boring and badly put together. The material was interesting enough, but the presentation was rubbish.

She found another, and another, and they were all the same. Then she found a brilliant one, easy to use, obvious, interesting.

And an idea dawned, edging over the horizon of her consciousness and flooding her with enthusiasm. But how?

She wanted it to be a secret, wanted to keep this to herself, so he didn't laugh at her or tease her or patronise her. She wasn't sure it would work—wasn't sure she could do it, although she couldn't be worse than some. But how? And where? She couldn't use his computer, he'd notice she'd been at his desk and want to know why.

No, she needed her own machine, but where? An office somewhere? Too expensive and, anyway, there was the dog to consider. She needed her own study here. If only there was a room she could use that Rob never went into…

Then she remembered the attic.

CHAPTER ONE

LAURIE felt the first twinges of failure with dismay.

Not again, she thought despairingly. We can't have failed again. *I* can't have failed again.

An hour later she was curled up on the sofa with the dog at her side, a low, gnawing ache eating at her, waiting for the phone to ring, for Rob to ask how she was.

Meaning *that,* of course.

She couldn't tell him again. She couldn't go through that same old ritual—are you all right? Do you want me to come home? I'll take you out for dinner tonight.

Why? To celebrate another wasted month?

She gave a humourless little laugh, just as the phone rang right on cue. She answered it on the second ring, injecting sparkle into her voice.

'How are you?' he asked without preamble. Pregnant yet?

'Fine. How are you?' she asked, ignoring the unspoken question. 'How's New York?'

'Cold and tedious. I'm stuck here for another week or two—problems. Can you manage?'

She almost laughed aloud. 'I expect so,' she said drily. God knows she was getting enough practice these days; he was hardly ever at home.

'I'll come back for the weekend if you like.'

'Why bother? Just press on and get home when you can,' she said, trying not to sound too unwelcoming. 'I'll be fine. I've got the dog for company.'

A man with less ego would have been offended, she thought, but Rob just chuckled. 'I'll speak to you tomorrow. You take care, now.'

Take care, just in case she might be pregnant.

Well, she wasn't—again.

She sighed and went up to the attic. Work called. She was over-run, too much to do, too little time. In the last year her secret business as a web designer had gone from nothing to an astonishing success. She worked from the moment Rob left the house to the moment he returned—well, a few moments before, if she could manage it, so she could slip into something elegant and create a little havoc in the kitchen so he'd think she'd been cooking all afternoon. It was amazing how many things she could produce now in less than half an hour.

She had no time to herself any longer, no time at all. Her friends had all but given up on her, because she kept fobbing them off with excuses, and one by one they'd drifted away. That was fine. She didn't need time for anything except this, the challenge she'd created for herself. The other challenge, the one she kept failing to meet, was harder because it was out of her control. Out of Rob's, too, and for the first time in his life he'd discovered something that money couldn't buy.

Well, it could, in a way. It could pay for expensive testing in private clinics, and IVF and other treatments till the cows came home, but in the end it might still be the same answer.

And anyway, as busy as she was, perhaps it was just as well. She wasn't sure how a baby would fit in, and she wasn't even sure she wanted one.

She stopped, her fingers coming to rest with a bump on the keys of the computer. A line of Xs appeared in front of her, and she lifted her hands and dropped them in her lap, stunned.

She didn't *want* a baby? Good grief. What a realisation. She thought about it, analysing the random thought that had dropped into her head as if from nowhere, and realised it was true. She didn't—not now, and maybe not ever. Not yet, at least. Not like this, with all the hassle of taking her temperature and phoning him at the office and having him drive home—he'd even flown back from Paris one time, to make love to her—make love? Huh, that was a joke.

They hadn't made real love in ages. More than a year. It had to be the right time, the right position—the right *angle,* for heaven's sake!—to maximise her chances of conceiving.

Well, she couldn't do it any more, and she wouldn't. Another realisation dawned. Not only did she not want a baby, she didn't want Rob's baby. She didn't want to be that tied to him, not now, when their marriage seemed to be a thing of habit rather than the joy it had been at first.

When had the gloss gone off? This year? Last?

When she'd failed to get pregnant immediately, she realised. A chill seemed to have crept in, a disappointment in each other, a sense of failure and perhaps reality. Their golden world had come to an end, and maybe there was nothing structural underneath to support them now.

She needed to think. Needed space and time to consider their relationship and their future—if they had such a thing. And she couldn't do that here.

Reaching for the keyboard again, she scrubbed what she'd been doing for the past few minutes, found a property website and clicked on Scotland. She loved

Scotland. She'd always loved it, ever since her childhood. Maybe she could think up there. Two estate agents came up. She chose the one in Inverness. It was further away than Edinburgh.

She jotted the phone number down on a Post-it note, then dialled with shaking fingers.

'I'm in a hurry to move to Scotland,' she told them. 'I don't need a mortgage—just somewhere small for me and the dog, with a home office if possible. Remote, if you can, and as cheap as possible but civilised. It must have heating and plumbing, though, and it needs a phone line.'

'Do you want to buy or rent?' the young lady asked. 'Only we've got a property that's just come on the books which sounds ideal, but they want to rent it just for a few months until they decide what to do.'

'Furnished or unfurnished?' Laurie asked, suddenly thinking of all the things she'd have to buy to equip a new home, and wondering if she was quite mad.

'Oh, furnished,' the agent told her. 'It's fully equipped and really lovely—two bedrooms, although at the moment you'd only have the use of one because they've put a lot of personal stuff in the second, but there's a room over the garage you could use as an office. They've gone to France and won't be back unless things don't work out, but it won't be very expensive even if they do sell it, not that far north. The only thing is, there's no guarantee it'll come up for sale.'

'That's no problem. It would help me now, at least. How far north?' she asked, her curiosity aroused.

'About an hour from here—near where Madonna was married. Near Tain, on the Dornock Firth. It's got wonderful distant sea and mountain views, if you don't mind the isolation.'

Mind? Just then she'd die for it. 'I'll take it,' she said instantly. 'When could I move?' Excitement was fizzing in her like champagne, the bubbles forming on the walls of her veins and tingling through them, bringing her to life.

'You haven't even seen the details!' the lady exclaimed, but Laurie had heard enough.

'What's it called?' she asked.

'Little Gluich.' She spelt it, and Laurie wrote it on the Post-it note next to the agent's number and stuck it on the wall over her desk.

'Can you fax me all the details?' she asked then, and within two hours it was set up, and she'd arranged to call in for the keys in two days' time.

All she had to do now was get there…

The house was empty.

Odd, how he knew that the moment he set foot over the threshold. The dog was missing, of course. That was a bit of a giveaway.

She must be walking him. At four-thirty, just barely into February? It was dark, or it would be soon. Not really safe on the roads. She'd probably gone over the fields instead, but it was very wet. In fact, he thought, remembering his drive home, it was pouring with rain.

She must be mad.

Unless she'd just found out she wasn't pregnant again. That made her do crazy things sometimes. Oh, lord, not again, he thought heavily. Poor Laurie.

He put the kettle on. She'd want tea when she got in. Tea and sympathy. Hell. He wasn't very good with the sympathy thing. He never seemed to hit the right note. In the meantime, he'd go and change out of his suit and put on something more relaxed. He'd been in a suit day in, day out for days. Weeks. Years?

The bedroom was very tidy. He'd obviously been away too long, he thought, unless Mrs Prewett had been today. Friday—or was it Thursday? He couldn't remember, and he wasn't sure now which days their cleaning lady came. He didn't think he could even remember what she looked like.

He scrubbed a hand tiredly through his hair and dropped onto the edge of the bed to pull off his shoes. Where was Laurie? It was dark now, the fingers of night creeping across the sky. Surely she wasn't walking the dog still? It would be dangerous in the wet and inky blackness.

He stood up and crossed to the window, peering down into the garden, but he couldn't see a thing. Could she have taken shelter in the summer house?

Unlikely. She would surely have run back to the house if she'd been caught in the rain.

Maybe she was in but hadn't heard him. The garage? No, he'd put his car away on the way in, and the electric zapper for the door also turned on the interior lights. He would have seen her, and anyway, why on earth would she be lurking in there in the dark, for heaven's sake? Besides, there was the dog. If he was here, he would have barked by now.

Unless she was at the vet with him, or staying with a friend. Maybe that was it. Maybe she'd been lonely and thought he wasn't coming back yet. He'd said he wasn't, in the end.

No. Her car was in the garage, what was he thinking

about? She didn't go anywhere on foot, except to walk the dog, because there was nowhere to go that was near enough.

So where *was* she?

He changed quickly and went downstairs, still puzzled. She should have left him a note, for heaven's sake.

Even though she wasn't expecting him? 'You're being ridiculous,' he muttered, conscious of a gnawing disappointment that she wasn't here to greet him. So much for surprising her!

Then common sense reared its mocking head, and he rang her mobile number.

He got the message service, and irritation edged into concern. He left a message, trying to sound casual.

'Darling, I'm home. Just wondered where you are. Ring me.'

He hung up, feeling a little aimless and lost. She was *always* here when he came home, and the house was dead and empty without her. He'd make tea. Maybe she'd be home by the time it was brewed. She might have gone out in a friend's car—perhaps to walk dogs together, and then back to the friend's for tea? They were probably out of range of the phone.

In Hertfordshire?

He paced to the window, glowering out into the impenetrable blackness of the wet night. It was truly foul out there. What if she was lying somewhere hurt?

Oh, God. Panic surged through him, and he pulled on his dogwalking coat and some wellies and went out into the garden, noting as he did that her coat and boots were missing. He called her as he tromped over the sodden grass, scanning round with the torch he'd taken with him. It hardly penetrated the gloom, and he didn't know where to start. The garden was more of a mini-wilderness, ten acres, many of them rough and wild and boggy, with lots of places where she could be lying out of sight.

The woodland? Oh, lord, the lake?

He crushed the panic and told himself not to over-react, and concentrated on calling the dog, over and over again, but there was nothing. After an hour he gave up and went back inside, ready to phone the police, and that was when he spotted the note.

It was stuck on the front of the fridge door, held by a magnet, and he pulled it off and opened the envelope with fingers numb with cold and wet.

'I've gone away for a while. I need to think. Don't worry, I'm fine. I'll ring. Laurie. PS. I have the dog.'

Rob stared at the paper, stunned. Gone away? To think? *Think?* About what, for God's sake?

The baby, he thought with a wave of sadness. The baby they couldn't seem to have. Oh, Laurie.

A lump formed in his throat and he swallowed it, hard. Where had she gone? What was she doing? She shouldn't be alone—

The phone rang, and he snatched it up and barked, 'Hello?'

'Rob, it's me. I just got your message. I didn't realise you were coming home yet.'

He stabbed a hand through his wet hair. 'Where the *hell* are you?' he snapped, his relief releasing his anger. 'I've been worried sick. I've been out in the rain and the dark scouring the garden with a torch—I've only just found your note. How come you haven't got the car—and what do you mean, think?'

'I've got another car.'

'What?' He sat down abruptly, stunned. 'What do you mean, you've got another car? That one's almost new!'

'I know. This is mine.'

Mine. Something about that word rang alarm bells in his head and he stared at the phone cautiously. 'The other one's yours.'

'Not in the same way. I don't want to talk about it. Anyway, I just wanted you to know I'm all right. I'll be in touch.' There was a soft click, and the burr of the dialling tone sounded in his ear.

'Laurie? Laurie, damn you, don't do this to me!' he yelled, and slammed the phone down, frustrated by his impotence.

Where was she? What was she doing?

Thinking.

What the hell did that mean, when it was at home? He phoned her again, and bombarded her with text messages, but to no avail. He was met by a relentless silence that nearly drove him crazy.

He paced round all evening, throwing together a scratch meal of bacon and eggs—about the only thing he could cook—and channel-hopped for a while, but the television couldn't hold his interest, so he had a hot shower and got ready for bed, but he was wide awake because it was still only five in the evening New York time, so he went into the study and went through some paperwork that was waiting for him.

And all the time he could see Laurie's face, a pale, perfect oval framed by that glorious soft, thick, shiny hair the colour of dark, moist peat. Her eyes were hazel, but when she was angry they fired gold and green sparks, and when she was aroused they went a wonderful soft smudgy green, and her mouth would yield to his touch, her lips swelling slightly and becoming rosy from his kisses, and afterwards her smile would be gentle and mellow and loving—

He frowned. She hadn't looked like that for a while. It had all lost its spontaneity, and the sparkle seemed to have gone out of their relationship.

What relationship? Apparently they didn't have one any more, he thought bitterly, slamming down the report unread. Damn her, where was she?

He left the study, prowling round the house, his temper fraying at the edges. He made a drink—just tea, he'd had too much alcohol and coffee in the past few days and he was feeling jaded and rough around the edges.

If only he could sleep, but there was no way. Between Laurie and the jet lag, he was stuffed. Maybe a long, hot soak in the bath would help. He went upstairs, and as he turned off the landing light a chink of light under the attic door caught his eye.

Someone must have left the light on—Laurie, probably, searching for a suitcase. He opened the door at the bottom of the narrow little stairs and reached for the switch, but the stream of gold came from further up. He nearly didn't bother, but something prompted him to go up.

There were three rooms up there, cluttered and untouched. The whole floor was filled with a load of old junk, really, things they'd bought and outgrown the need for, old family things they didn't have the heart to throw out. He hadn't been up here in months—years, probably. He never needed to.

But someone had, because everything had been cleared out of one of the rooms, and it was almost empty.

Empty, except for a desk, a chair, a filing cabinet and a telephone—and a dangling flex with a bare, glowing bulb on the end.

He stared round, utterly confused, and slowly crossed to the chair, running his fingers thoughtfully over the back of it. It was his old desk chair, too upright to sit at for long, but ideal for working at the computer. Better than the one he had now, in fact, although not as good looking.

Still, that wasn't everything.

He looked around at the room, puzzled. It looked like an empty office after a business had moved out. Odd scraps of paper here and there, barren and lifeless, the heart gone out of it.

He sat down and went through the desk drawers, but they were empty. The filing cabinet?

Also empty. He checked the bin, but all there was in it was a bit of stamp edging and an old envelope with a frank mark on it—a frank of a firm in Scotland.

William Guthrie Estate Agents, Inverness.

Estate agents? Why was she corresponding with estate agents?

Unless it was a clue to her whereabouts—

He tore the place apart, searching every nook and cranny again, and then pulled the desk out from the wall. Nothing. Then, behind the filing cabinet, he saw a sheet of paper.

His hand wouldn't fit, so he grasped the cabinet and shifted it, then plucked the paper from its hiding place. It was dusty and wrinkled, handwritten, a mass of jottings and calculations of figures. Figures that looked like the turnover of a business. Figures that made him blink.

Laurie's business?

Doing what? Maybe she was working as a homefinder? Hence the letter from the estate agents. No. She'd never earn that much.

He glanced at the back of the desk, and there, suspended halfway down the back of it, hanging by a corner, was a yellow sticky note. He peeled it off, and sat down on the desk thoughtfully.

William Guthrie, it read, and a number, and jotted below were the words 'Little Gluich'.

A house? Had she for God's sake bought a house in Inverness?

With what?

He looked again at the figures on the sheet of paper, and shook his head slowly. With that, maybe. With her apparently very healthy income. Unless she was renting.

He looked at his watch. Ten minutes past midnight. Almost nine hours to kill before he could reasonably ring the estate agents and find out what the hell was going on.

If they'd tell him, of course, which was by no means a foregone conclusion. He'd have to play the guileless, rather daffy husband, and just see how much he could get out of them. He'd play it by ear.

Unless, of course, he made a personal visit. He glanced at his watch again. He wouldn't sleep, not a chance, and by the time he'd phoned Luton and booked a flight, driven over there and hung around, then hired a car at the other end and driven to Inverness, it would be nearly as quick to drive.

He took the little yellow note and the envelope and the calculations, flicked off the lights and went into his room, tipping his suitcase out ruthlessly on the bed and repacking. He'd need wash things, a towel perhaps, and thick, warm clothes. Nothing too formal, and nothing much. He didn't intend to be there long.

He left the house before twelve-thirty, wondering whether he was chasing about the countryside after a total red herring, but he couldn't just sit there and twiddle his thumbs. He needed to see her, and he needed to see her now.

He hit the almost deserted A1 within minutes, and headed north, pulling over at Scotch Corner for coffee at five, then pressing on again. It got much slower in the rush hour, and he reached the outskirts of Edinburgh and stopped briefly for a late breakfast, stocking up on enough coffee to keep him awake and making Inverness by one.

He parked the car in a multi-storey and asked someone the way to the estate agents, then wound his way through the streets until he found it.

He caught a glimpse of himself in the window as he entered the office. He looked shattered, his eyes red-rimmed, his mouth a grim line. Good grief. If he didn't lighten up, they'd think he was an axe-murderer! He forced his shoulders to relax as he pushed the door open and went in.

The office was almost deserted. A young woman sitting behind a desk looked up with a friendly smile. 'Good afternoon, sir. Can I help you?'

He dropped into the chair opposite her and treated her to his most persuasive confused-little-boy grin. 'I hope so. I've driven all the way here from London to join my wife, and I can't find the directions she left me. They must have fallen out of the car door pocket when I stopped for breakfast. She's just taken on a property from you—at least, I hope it was you. Your name rings a bell. I hope I won't have to trawl round all the agents.'

He dragged a hand through his hair and tried to look as if everything was against him. Not hard, under the circumstances.

'What was the name, sir?' she asked him, and his heart thumped with anticipation. So far, so good. She hadn't told him it was confidential information and sent him packing, at least.

'Ferguson. She moved very recently—the last couple of days. I feel such an idiot for losing the directions—I'll blame it on the jet lag. I've just got back from New York,' he explained with a rueful smile. Maybe she'd fall for the exhaustion theory and feel sorry for him.

Or not. She was shaking her head. 'Ferguson—that doesn't ring a bell, sir, I'm sorry.'

He thought rapidly. 'How about her maiden name? She sometimes uses it for business,' he lied wildly. 'Laurie Taylor. I think the property's called Little something.'

The woman's face cleared. 'Oh, yes, of course, Ms Taylor. She picked up the keys of Little Gluich yesterday morning. I couldn't forget her—she had a dog with her, a real teddybear.'

He pulled a wry face. 'That's right—Midas—our golden retriever. He's a bit friendly, I'm afraid.'

She laughed, mellowing, and Rob realised with grim satisfaction that she was falling for his charm. Just give me the directions, he thought desperately, before someone with more sense of client confidentiality emerges from the woodwork and everything grinds to a halt.

'No problem, Mr Ferguson,' she said with a smile, and he felt relief course through him. 'I think we've still got a copy of the details we prepared, they'll have the directions on. Here. It's a lovely little property—really cosy. I hope you find it all right. Give us a ring if not and speak to Mr Guthrie when he comes back from his lunch break.'

She handed him a set of details from the filing cabinet and smiled again, her face dimpling. She was a sweetheart—totally out of order giving him the information, but a sweetheart for all that. He could have hugged her, but thought better of it.

'You're a lifesaver,' he told her. 'I tried to ring but I couldn't get her on the mobile, and I don't even know if she's got the phone connected at the house. All that fell out of the door with the directions.'

He smiled again, treating her to the full wattage, and she went pink and dimpled again. The phone rang, and with an apologetic smile she turned to answer it. He made his escape, heading back to the car park with a geographical instinct honed over years of visiting strange places, then slid behind the wheel and opened the slim folder containing the information he was after.

It looked charming, he thought. A little croft house, white-painted, snuggled down in a crease in the hillside with a glimpse of the sea in the distance. No wonder it had appealed to her. He wondered what Little Gluich meant. Nothing, probably.

He read the directions, located it on his road atlas and pulled out of the car park. Just one more hour, and he'd be with her.

He wound his way north, crossing an estuary on a bridge—the Firth of something. Cromarty? Moray? One or the other. Cromarty, he thought. He'd done Moray on the way out of Inverness. He saw seals swimming off the shore and more basking on rocks near the wreck of a ship, then turned north again onto a little road that headed over the hills towards Tain.

And there it was, or at least there the turning was. He couldn't see the house from the road, there was a kink in the hill, but he turned down the track and winced as his car grounded on the *stony* grassy hummock in the middle.

Tough. He lurched and bumped his way down, and round a little bend, and there it was, a thin plume of smoke curling from the chimney in welcome. A car was outside—nothing flashy, nothing like the BMW in the garage at home, but *hers,* as she'd put it.

He felt a flutter in his chest as the adrenaline kicked in. Fight or flight?

He'd never backed away from anything in his life, and he wasn't starting now. He wanted his wife back, and he was going to have her.

All he had to do was talk her into it…

CHAPTER TWO

SHE heard the car before she saw it, grinding slowly down the track towards the house and disturbing the peace and tranquillity of her little hideaway.

A neighbour, come to welcome her? The postman?

From her vantage point in the office over the garage, she peered down at the drive a little warily. 'Who is it, Midas?' she asked, her voice instinctively lowered, and the dog whined and stood up on his back legs, his front paws on the windowsill, and watched with her.

The ghostly silver bonnet of Rob's Mercedes nosed through the gateway, its headlights gleaming dully in the fading light, and her heart sank as the car crunched over the gravel and came to rest beside her much more modest Ford.

How on earth had he found her? She'd been so careful, cleared everything away without trace, or so she'd thought. Even the attic she'd left spotless—hadn't she? There must have been something lying around, some little clue. Blast. She'd always known he'd find her in the end, because he didn't give up on anything, but she had hoped for a few more days—maybe even weeks—to sort her thoughts out.

And now he was here. Still, maybe he'd ring the bell and go away if she didn't show herself. Her heart pounding, she sank back away from the window and grabbed the dog's collar, pulling him down beside her. He whined in protest and tried to jump up again, but she hung on tight.

'Midas, no,' she whispered. 'Be quiet, there's a good boy.'

He whined again, recognising the sound of the car, and she wrapped her hand round his muzzle and stroked him with the other hand, trying to calm him. 'Good boy. Hush now. Maybe he'll go away.'

She snorted softly under her breath. Not a chance, and the dog knew it. Just in case, though, he was determined to bark a greeting, and she had to hang on to his muzzle and pet him constantly to keep him quiet. Still, at least she hadn't got the lights on in the office, although the glow from the computer was probably visible. She reached out a hand and switched off the monitor, and her little office sank into gloom. Heavens, it was later than she'd realised, but she'd been so busy.

Edging up to the window, she peered down onto the drive and watched.

Rob got out of the car and straightened, then looked around, his eyes narrowed, scanning for clues. First he checked out her car, then he went over to the cottage and knocked on the door before turning the handle and going in.

Damn him! she thought, fuming. How *dare* he just walk into her house! She crossed to the other side of the room, peeping through the roof-light to get a better view.

She could see him going from room to room, flicking lights on, prowling. She imagined him fingering the things left by the owners, things he'd never seen before. She'd hardly been here long enough to put her stamp on anything except the bedroom and bathroom. Everywhere else was just as she'd found it, because she'd brought practically nothing with her yesterday except the contents of her office, a few clothes and the dog.

She'd wanted to get away from her old life, have a fresh start, and now he was all over it, touching it, imprinting himself on it so it would no longer be hers alone, the safe haven she'd wanted it to be.

Safe haven? What was she thinking about? He was hardly dangerous! She made it sound like he was a serial killer instead of her husband of five years. She must be going crazy. But even so, she felt somehow violated.

No. That was too strong. Invaded, then.

She watched him moving around, doing his tour of inspection. It didn't take long. There were only the two rooms downstairs, one at each end, and the stairs running from side to side with the bathroom behind them. Above were two bedrooms, hers and the store, and a big cupboard full of all sorts.

Surely to goodness he couldn't be much longer, she thought, the adrenaline surging through her body and making her heart race.

He wasn't. He emerged from the front door, shrugging down inside his coat collar against the bitter wind, and she moved back a little from the window, her heart pounding with suspense. Maybe he'd think he'd come to the wrong house and would go away.

Or not.

He looked up at the window, his eyes seeming to fix on her face, and even from this distance she could see their piercing cobalt blue. She shrank back into the shadows, getting a better grip on the wiggling dog.

He could hear his master coming, hear the crunch of footsteps on the stones and the squeak of the handle as the door opened at the bottom of the stairs. A blast of icy air invaded their cosy little hideaway and Midas whimpered and squirmed in her hands.

The stairs creaked under a firm, steady tread, and Rob's head appeared over the top step, his eyes assessing.

'Hello, Laurie,' he said, and the dog, displaying a singular lack of judgement, hurled himself out of her arms and hit him in mid chest.

He staggered back, righted himself against the wall and ruffled the dog's fur affectionately while Laurie tried to quell the thundering of her heart and compose herself to deal with him without hysterics.

'Hello, mutt,' he said, pushing the dog down out of the way and climbing the last few stairs. He looked around, his eyes like twin blue lasers scanning the sophisticated computer equipment, the notes pinned up on the wall, the collection of mugs by the keyboard.

'Nice little place you've got here,' he said blandly, but it didn't fool her for a second. She wondered what the chances were of her hustling him out before it was too late.

Huh. It was already too late. She sat down in front of the computer, blocking his view of her desk, or trying to.

'What are you doing here?' she asked, trying to keep her voice calm and not give in to the anger building in her. Why couldn't he have just left her alone? He knew she was all right, she'd only just spoken to him less than twenty-four hours ago! Why come here to persecute her?

'Interesting set-up,' he said, ignoring her question and continuing his inspection of her pinboard. 'What's the business?'

'Mine,' she said, not willing to share even the nature

of her business with him, never mind the intimate details he'd try and winkle out of her. 'It's mine, and it's private. I repeat, what are you doing here, Rob?'

His eyes met hers, red rimmed with exhaustion but determined, the blue of his irises touched with flint. 'I would have thought it was obvious what I was doing here. I've come to take you home,' he said softly, and her traitorous heart kicked against her ribs.

She snorted. 'Not a chance. I told you, I want to think.'

'You can think at home.'

'No, I can't. I just want this time to myself. You should have rung, you've had a wasted journey. I've got nothing to say to you at the moment, and I want you out of here. This is my house, my office, my life.'

'And you're my wife.'

'Am I?' she asked bluntly, and he recoiled a fraction, as if she'd struck a painful blow. Good, she thought, ruthlessly crushing her guilt. She was fed up with him taking her for granted. She stood up, gathering the cups together and standing waiting by the top of the stairs. She gestured for him to go down, but he just smiled and took her chair at the desk, turning on the monitor and tapping keys on her computer and opening files, flicking through her personal business with ridiculous ease and a casual disregard for her privacy.

'Leave it alone! That's nothing to do with you,' she fumed, ready to dump the dregs of the cups on his head, and he spun round in the chair and fixed her with those piercing eyes.

'You're a web designer,' he said slowly.

'Ten out of ten. Out.'

He unfolded himself from the desk and stepped closer,

looking down into her face searchingly. 'There was no need for you to leave. You could have told me you wanted to do it,' he said, his voice seductive, almost convincing.

'I wanted it to be mine,' she said, and he gave a tiny huff of laughter.

'Mine again. You seem to be using that word a lot. Whatever happened to ours?'

'Yours, you mean.'

His eyes narrowed and he searched her face, then shrugged. 'I don't know what's eating you, Laurie, but we'll talk about it when you come home.'

'I'm not coming home,' she repeated emphatically, but he just smiled.

'Oh, I think you are.'

That was it. She lost it. Without another thought, she dumped the contents of the mugs on his head and stomped off down the stairs, leaving him swearing under his breath and brushing ineffectually at his clothes. A smile tugged at her mouth, but she suppressed it. It was a childish thing to have done, but he'd provoked her beyond endurance, and she wasn't going to laugh it off. God forbid he should think she wasn't serious about this. She was done being dictated to.

He was right behind her, his temper barely under control, and she felt a tiny frisson of anticipation. She hadn't seen him really angry for ages, but she knew she could trust him not to hurt her, and right then she was spoiling for a fight.

She marched over to the cottage, just half a stride ahead of him, and he was through the door behind her before she had time to slam it in his face.

'It won't work, Laurie,' he said grimly, following her

into the kitchen with the dog at his heels. 'I'm not going without you.'

'Well, I'm not going, and you're not staying, so it's going to be a bit tricky, really, isn't it?'

'I mean it,' he said, his voice taut with determination, all that earlier gentle coaxing gone, banished no doubt by the coffee dregs in his hair and the cold bite of the wind and her failure to succumb to his authority. 'I'm not just walking away from this,' he went on. 'You're my wife, and if you think you can just run off like this without talking about it, you're mistaken.'

'I hardly ran off.'

'No? Then why didn't you tell me where you were going, and what you were doing? And what the hell is this business you've been running in the attic of my house without telling me? How long's it been going on?'

'*Our* house, I think, and don't you mean asking your permission?' she snapped, whirling on him, her temper finally frayed beyond endurance. 'Don't you mean what the hell was I doing *sneaking around behind your back daring to have a life?*'

'Don't be ridiculous,' he retorted. 'Of course you can have a life.'

'Just so long as it includes playing hostess to your incredibly boring business acquaintances with monotonous regularity, and dressing up in pretty clothes to be the elegant little social butterfly I'm expected to be. God forbid I should wear jeans.'

'You can wear jeans.'

'Versace jeans,' she snorted, whirling away again to dump the mugs in the sink before she hurled them at him. 'Not ordinary jeans from the discount shop on the corner.'

'You've never worn jeans like that! You don't even *like* jeans,' he protested, and she felt a pang of guilt. He was quite right, she hadn't ever bought cheap jeans, or any cheap clothes in fact, and she wouldn't want to. She just wanted the *right* to, that was all.

She turned back to the sink, washing the mugs for something to do that didn't involve screaming with frustration.

He sighed, a harsh exhalation filled with the same frustration and irritation that she was feeling. I must be getting to him, she thought in satisfaction. There's a miracle.

She turned round, just as he hooked out a chair from the table and dropped wearily into it. His eyes were tired and red-rimmed, his face was drawn, and she remembered he'd been travelling now for over twenty-four hours.

He didn't have to come up here after me, she reminded herself. It was his choice. Then a little dribble of stale coffee trickled off his hair and down his temple and dripped onto his coat, and she felt a twinge of guilt. It was a lovely navy cashmere coat, only a few weeks old and hideously expensive, and the splash of coffee over one shoulder and down the front did nothing to enhance it. Her guilt prompted a partial climb-down.

'I'll make you tea, then you can go,' she conceded.

She waited for a second, but instead of repeating his intention to stay he merely settled back, folded his arms across his chest and smiled.

Rats. He looked so sexy when he did that, sexy enough to distract her—but only for a moment. She reminded herself of all the reasons why she was here—his autocratic behaviour, his expectations of her, the time he spent away from home when she was left holding the fort.

Holding the baby? She shuddered to think what would have happened if she'd conceived. Would he have come home at all, without the need to attempt to impregnate her at regular intervals?

No, there was no way she was going back to him. Not yet, at least, and maybe not ever.

Even if he did have the sexiest eyes she'd ever seen. She'd fallen for them years ago. She wasn't falling for them again.

Oh, no…

She was a web designer. He was amazed, although he shouldn't have been. If he'd given it a moment's thought, he would have realised that sitting at home with only the dog for company while she waited to see if she was pregnant wouldn't be enough for her. She was too bright, far too bright and full of imagination and life and restless invention.

In the past two years since she'd given up work and settled down to wait for the baby that hadn't come, she'd redone the house from end to end, got Midas from a rescue centre and turned him from a cowering, gangly pup into a bright and confident dog who was her devoted companion, and sorted out the grounds of the house with the help of an army of skilled gardeners and landscapers.

That accomplished, he must have been crazy to imagine she would then settle down to wait for maternity to catch up with her.

Not Laurie. Of course she'd needed something to do.

But to do it in secret, without sharing it with him—that rankled. Hurt, in fact, he thought in surprise. He wondered when things had started to go wrong, and realised with shock that he hadn't even noticed that they had until now, when he'd thought about it and remembered what it used to be like between them.

Things had gone wrong, though, or she wouldn't be here now, hundreds of miles from home, making him tea before she threw him out on his ear. Well, tough. He wasn't going, not till this was sorted out, and it looked like the weather was playing right into his hands.

A quick glance at the window showed that night had fallen while they'd been talking, the clouds so thick and full they'd snuffed out the last of the daylight.

He stood up and swished the little curtains shut at the single window, blocking out the view of the snowflakes that were starting to whirl against the glass. In an hour, with any luck, it would be falling too thick and fast to allow him to venture out, so he'd have to stay.

They might be snowed in for days…

He felt his body stir. He'd missed her. It had been a couple of weeks since he'd seen her last, and a little making up would be fun. Hiding a smile of satisfaction, he settled back in the chair, picked up the mug of tea she pushed towards him and prepared to wait her out.

It infuriated her when he did that.

Sat there, with his tea propped on his belt buckle, a patient look on his face, and said nothing.

She hated silence. She always had, and he knew it. Of all the things he did that got her mad, this was the worst.

She promised herself she wouldn't rise, not this time. Picking up her own tea, she changed the subject from her to him. 'How was New York?' she asked, as if they were sitting in their own kitchen and she hadn't just walked out on him and moved to the other end of the British Isles.

He didn't twitch an eyebrow, to his credit, but then he was a very successful businessman and used to hiding his reactions.

'Cold, dull. I missed you.'

If only that were true, she thought sadly, remembering the times he'd gone away at first and how glad she'd been to have him back—how eagerly she'd welcomed him.

But recently…

'How's Mike?' she asked, enquiring after the New York partner who handled most of the North American business, and refusing to rise to the bait.

'All right. He asked how you were.'

'And what did you tell him?'

He smiled, a slight hitch of one side of his mouth, not really a smile so much as a grimace. 'I told him you were fine,' he said softly.

She looked away. She couldn't face down those piercing, all-seeing eyes. He was too good at boardroom games. She should know. She'd played them with him only a few years ago, before she'd 'retired' from active involvement in his business ventures and settled back to wait for the baby.

She sighed and sipped her tea, wishing he would go away and knowing full well he wouldn't, not at least without a promise from her to come home—a promise she couldn't make. 'When did you get back?' she asked, wondering about his jet lag and if he'd had any sleep.

'Yesterday afternoon. I was home just after four.' The

unspoken reproach hung in the air and irritated her into retaliation.

'I didn't *know* you were coming back yesterday.'

'No, of course not,' he said, and then continued with mild reproach. 'Not that you were there to take my call—'

'I don't have to be there twenty-four hours a day,' she reminded him sharply, and his eyebrow quirked up in response.

'Of course you don't,' he said soothingly. 'But you know my mobile number, and I do think that you could perhaps have done more than leave a note before you walked out on our relationship.'

There was no attempt now to hide the reproach, his voice hardening and showing, for the first time, his true feelings. Good. She could deal with that. She couldn't deal with the bland, expressionless board-room persona he'd been conveying for the past few minutes. And if he was angry, then maybe he cared, and maybe, just maybe, there was hope for them.

'I didn't walk out on our relationship, I just wanted a little space,' she reminded him.

'I would have given you space if you'd asked for it. You could have said so. You know you only have to ask for anything.'

'Maybe I didn't want to ask. Maybe I'm sick of asking for everything.'

'Sick of sharing?'

'We don't share,' she told him flatly. 'We hardly share anything any more. I'm amazed you noticed I wasn't there—'

'Don't be ridiculous, of course I noticed.'

'Yes, you would have had to pour your own drink, make your own supper. Poor little lamb.'

He growled under his breath, and she buried her nose in her mug and ignored him.

'You could have said something, discussed it with me,' he went on, hammering home the point.

'And have you brush it aside? Or trivialise it? Patronise me with another of your "you don't want to do that" lectures? I didn't want that, Rob. I wanted to think—to have time to work out in my own mind just how I feel about us, before it's too late.'

'Too late?'

'Yes, too late. Before we become locked together irretrievably into parenthood. I want to be sure I want your baby before I conceive, and at the moment I'm not sure—not sure at all, about any of it.'

'I take it you're not pregnant, then, again,' he said cautiously, putting her hackles up.

'No, I'm not damn well pregnant. I don't *get* pregnant, remember, so all this might be academic anyway—'

'And the business?' he said smoothly, moving on without drawing breath. 'How long have you been running that? A year? Eighteen months?'

'Nearly a year.'

'A year. You've been running it for a year—successfully, by all indications—and yet you didn't think to mention it.'

She had. Over and over again, she'd nearly told him, but it had never seemed like the right time.

'You're always too busy, or away, or we're entertaining. There's never been a good time,' she told him. 'We never have time to talk.'

'In a year?'

She sighed shortly. 'Rob, you've been away—and when you've been home—' All he'd done was try and get her pregnant. But she couldn't say that, so she shrugged and shook her head and gave up. Not Rob, though. He didn't give up.

He settled back and folded his arms and gave her a level look. 'I'm not too busy now. You want to talk about it, tell me about it now. I've got nothing else to do.'

'Yes, you have. You're going,' she told him, standing up and taking his half-full cup from his hand and tipping it into the sink.

That brow arched again. 'I don't think so.'

'Tough.'

'It is. Look out of the window. I'm going nowhere.'

She opened the curtain and pressed her face to the glass, but all she could see was swirling white. Snow, for heavens sake! That was all she needed.

'It's just a little flurry. It'll pass,' she said with more confidence than she felt. 'You'll easily get to the village. There's a bed and breakfast there. You can stay there for the night and set off back to London tomorrow.'

She snapped on the outside light, yanked open the front door and a blast of snow and arctic wind drove her back into the house. She slammed the door with difficulty and turned to lean on it, frustration threatening to overwhelm her. There was no way he could drive in that. She couldn't see anything except a wall of white. Even finding the car would be a nightmare.

Oh, damn, she thought. They had no choice—he could die out there, and whatever was wrong with their relationship, she didn't hate him that much—if at all.

'All right, you can stay,' she said grudgingly, then

added with as much firmness as she could muster, 'but you'll have to sleep in the sitting room, you aren't sharing with me.'

He gave a soft snort. 'Don't be ridiculous,' he reasoned. 'We're married. We've slept together for five years. What difference can one more night make?'

Plenty to me, she thought, knowing her own weakness for his charm and knowing quite well that he'd turn it up full to get her back, if that was what he wanted. He'd seduce her—win her round, talk her into going back. No, it was too dangerous to let him that near.

'Either you sleep in the sitting room, or you go,' she said flatly, avoiding answering his question.

'Fine,' he said, and she did a mental double take. It wasn't like him to back down so uncharacteristically fast—if at all! He settled back into the chair and folded his arms. 'Any more tea?'

His eyes were wide and innocent, but she knew better. There was nothing innocent about Rob—never had been, never would be. She didn't trust him not to use that charm ruthlessly just the moment it suited him, but she was stuck. There was nowhere to go, no escape. They were trapped together, and it was going to take a massive effort of will not to allow herself to succumb.

But she was going to do it. Come hell or high water, she was going to do it, and that was that.

End of conversation.

Somehow...!

CHAPTER THREE

IT WAS bitterly cold. It took Rob five minutes to find the car, collect his case and mobile phone and get back into the cottage, after making a detour at Laurie's request to shut down her computer and lock the garage and set the alarm.

She was going to do it herself, but he'd overruled her on that one. There was no way he was letting her go out there in the teeth of the blizzard that was raging all around them, and for one rather disturbing minute he himself hadn't been able to find his way back to the cottage. He'd wondered in an oddly detached way if he was destined to perish out there on the barren Scottish hillside, but then the snow had eased and he'd seen the dull gleam of the outside light, and he'd realised he'd been going the wrong way.

So easily done in the confusing swirl of snow, but a mistake that could have proved fatal under other circumstances, he thought. He felt a dawning respect for the wild and tempestuous elements and the men that braved them on a daily basis. Quite where such a blizzard had come from he couldn't imagine, but it had, apparently out of nowhere, and it was threatening to tear the roof off the house.

He turned the handle on the door, to have it almost snatched out of his hand by the wind. He shut it by throwing his weight against it, and as he stood inside it and listened to the raging storm outside, he wondered why on earth people chose to mount polar expeditions. Mad, the lot of them, he thought, brushing the snow off his shoulders and tousling his hair to shake the wet out of it.

'Here, let me take that,' Laurie said, peeling his coat off his back and flapping it firmly. 'Come into the sitting room—the fire's lit and I've revved it up a bit. I'll make you a hot drink.'

He didn't argue. It was rather nice being waited on by her, although not entirely necessary. It made him feel a bit like one of the old hunter-gatherers, being welcomed home by his mate at the end of a hunting expedition—except that he'd only gone fifty feet to the car and back, and his quarry had been a very co-operative suitcase.

The mate was a bit grudging, too. Ah, well.

He chuckled wearily under his breath. The jet lag must be getting to him, addling his brain. He sat down in front of the fire, stretched out his legs towards the warmth and sighed with contentment. So good. Warm. Comfortable. Peaceful.

Within seconds he was asleep.

That was where Laurie found him, two minutes later, when she came back in with two cups of tea and some cake on a tray.

She set it down silently, then curled up in the chair by the side of the fire with her tea and watched him sleep. He looked exhausted, she realised. Exhausted and thinner, run to a frazzle. He was doing too much. He'd been doing too much for more than a year, but he wouldn't even discuss it.

He did what was necessary, that was all, he said. Nothing more, nothing less. End of discussion.

It was funny, they used to discuss things a lot, but just recently she felt he'd been stonewalling her. Maybe it was just her imagination. Maybe he was just too busy to talk, and too tired to bother.

Too tired to do anything—except a hasty flurry of activity every few weeks, in a vain attempt to get her pregnant.

She felt the hot sting of tears behind her eyes, and blinked them away. They'd lost so much. They'd been so happy at first, happy and full of life and enthusiasm. Nothing had been too much trouble, too much effort, too much of a challenge.

They'd talked and argued and made up, laughed and cried together, shared everything.

And now—now they had nothing except the spectre of failure in their most personal lives, and jet lag. She rested her head on the back of the chair and gave a quiet sigh. She'd needed this time out so much. She hadn't realised how much until she'd agreed to take the cottage, and she'd felt a huge weight off her shoulders.

Freedom, she'd thought. Freedom from unspoken criticism, from failure, from Rob's expectations of her as a hostess, from her friends' expectations of her as a shopping companion and marriage counsellor—that was the funny one, she thought.

Andy asking her for advice on her marriage, when her own marriage was in such disarray.

Something splashed on her hand—a tear, she realised in surprise. She blinked and sniffed, but another one fell to join the first, and another, so she just lay there with her head against the back of the chair and let them fall.

She cried silently. She'd grown used to doing it while Rob slept, it was nothing new to her, but she didn't usually do it with the lights on so he could see her if he woke.

Still, there was no danger he'd wake now. He was exhausted, and even he didn't catch up with his sleep that quickly. She closed her eyes, rested her hand on the dog's shaggy head at her knee and waited for the tears to stop. They would in the end. They always did.

She'd been crying.

He lay there, sprawled out on the sofa, and watched her without moving. There were tears drying on her cheeks, long salty tracks down the pale, smooth skin, and he felt his heart contract.

Oh, Laurie. He wanted to hold her, to comfort her, but he didn't know how, or even if he could. What could he say that would make any difference?

Nothing. It was probably him she was crying about—or them, at least. He felt sick. How long had she felt like this, so sad inside that she could sit and cry silently while he slept?

Had she done it before, maybe in their big, high bed in the lovely house he'd thought was their home? Had he slept beside her, oblivious to her misery?

And yet he still didn't know what he'd done, or what was wrong. Until today he would have said she was crying because she couldn't conceive, but now he wasn't so sure.

Was she having an affair? It was possible. Maybe her failure to conceive was deliberate. Perhaps she was on the Pill, or maybe her reluctance to have any tests was because she was happy as things were and didn't want a child.

She'd said something about that in the kitchen. He hadn't really taken it in at the time. He'd thought she was just trying to console herself, but maybe she really meant it. Maybe she didn't want a child—or at least, not his.

It was a sobering thought. He lay there and let it sink in, slowly absorbing the implications. It seemed there was far more to her unscheduled disappearance than a simple flounce or a cry for attention. She really seemed to have deep, fundamental doubts about their relationship, and he realised he was going to have to listen to her, to talk it through rather than simply cajole her into returning home. For the first time he felt a seed of doubt that he would win her back, and something deep inside him clenched with fear.

He watched her sleep, the tears slowly drying on her cheeks, her hand hanging over the edge of the chair above the dog's head. He was lying against the front of the chair, his nose on his paws, as if he'd just sunk down there from sitting under her hand. His eyes were closed, but Rob knew he was alert. One move from her and he'd be up.

He was her devoted slave, and Rob felt an irrational pang of jealousy. Not that he'd want to be her devoted slave, far from it, but he wouldn't mind going back to the lively and productive partnership they'd had before.

She'd been so vital and alive, so funny, so sharp and quick-witted. He supposed she still was, but the vital spark seemed to have gone, extinguished by something he didn't really understand.

He remembered the first time he'd met her, at Julia

and Charlie's wedding. He'd been Charlie's best man, and she'd been the chief bridesmaid. He'd felt his heart kick then, seeing her behind Julia, and then during the reception he'd talked to her and got to know her a little, and discovered that not only was she very beautiful, she was also clever.

She had a mind, a sharp and incisive mind and the verbal ability to go with it, and they'd wrangled about everything from fashion to the state of the stock market.

'So what do you do for a living?' he'd asked, and she'd laughed wryly.

'At the moment I'm temping in an office, but my secretarial skills are slight and that's a bit of problem in the job I'm covering, so it won't last long, but I have to eat and run my car and pay off my uni debts, so I can't afford to be picky. I'm looking around, though, waiting for the right thing to come up. I'd like a job with a bit of responsibility—something to get my teeth into. I'm just bored to death at the moment.'

Without pausing to analyse his motives, he slipped his hand into his pocket and pulled out his wallet, then handed her one of his cards. 'Here. Ring me. There might be something—I don't know what, but we've always got room for good people. I'll have a chat with my Human Resources team. Come in and see us.'

She looked at the card, plucked at the sides of her pretty, floaty bridesmaid's dress with a smile and then tucked the card down the low front of her bodice, into her bra. He caught sight of a peep of pale ivory lace against pale ivory breast, and hot blood surged in his veins.

'I knew having boobs would come in useful one day,' she said with a throaty chuckle, and he had to shut his eyes and count to ten. He could think of all sorts of uses for her soft, full, ripe breasts, and tucking business cards into them was way down the list.

Unless he was doing the tucking…

The next time he saw her was a week later, and she was dressed in a demure business suit with a high-necked blouse, but he could still see the firm, ripe swell of her breasts in his mind and he had to force himself to concentrate on interviewing her.

Within moments he'd forgotten about her body and was fascinated by her mind, instead. They talked about the business, about investment analysis and the stock market and maintaining the right sort of client base, and he was amazed. Most of the women he knew of her age would have been totally out of their depth, or bored to death.

Not Laurie Taylor. She had views and opinions, and she wasn't frightened to express them. They argued, they tore holes in each other's arguments, and in the end they agreed to differ.

For a moment, then, her confidence had seemed to falter, as if by disagreeing with him she thought she'd blown the interview, but then he'd smiled and held out his hand.

'Welcome to the team—if you'll come?'

'You mean you want me, after all that?' she'd said, surprise in her voice and her eyes, and he'd smiled back.

Oh, yes, he thought, I want you. *Do I want you!*

'You're too good to pass up,' he said. 'I like the way you think.'

'But you don't agree with me.'

He smiled again. 'But I can argue with you, and you don't take offence. That's very useful—helps me main-tain a wider perspective. I think we need a new post. I'll have an assistant—it's probably about time. How much do you want?'

She laughed softly. 'How much do you think I'm worth?'

He thought of a figure and doubled it, and she blinked.

'Is that a yes?'

'Absolutely.' She gulped and nodded, and he just hoped she was worth it.

She was. By the end of the first week he wondered how he'd coped without her. By the end of the first month, their relationship had become more personal. Their wrangling over business issues had taken on the quality of a challenge—almost a game—and the stakes were rising.

One day, after a particularly long-running argument proved her right and him wrong, she crowed with delight and danced round the office, and he was suddenly, shockingly aroused.

'OK,' he said, retreating behind his desk for the sake of modesty. 'I'll concede—'

'Concede? You're mad! I've won—'

'I'll concede,' he repeated with a slow smile, 'on condition you have dinner with me. A sort of forfeit.'

She cocked her head on one side, hands on hips, sassy and luscious. 'I thought you paid the forfeit if you lost.'

'You do,' he said, thinking quickly. 'I lost. I have to pay.'

Her head tilted the other way. 'I'll want a good dinner—not just any old place.'

He gave a rueful laugh. 'I never doubted it for a moment,' he murmured. 'So—are we on?'

She pretended to think for a moment, one luminous

pink fingertip pressed against her pursed lips, then she sparkled and laughed. 'We're on,' she said, and perched on the edge of the desk unconsciously revealing a great length of thigh. 'So—where are we going?'

'Don't know yet. Dress up.'

'Long? Short?'

'Long,' he said, knowing he wouldn't get through the evening if he had to look at her legs, but his clever ruse didn't work, because her gown was slit to the thigh and her sparkly, slinky tights were nearly the death of him.

'Just do me one favour,' he said as the waiter left them contemplating the menu. 'Let's not talk about work. I really, really don't want to fight.'

She grinned. 'OK. We'll talk about you. How did you get to know Charlie?' she asked, and so he told her about his childhood at boarding school, and then asked her about her childhood and was rewarded by tales of scrapes and close shaves, all the naughty little things that children did, but recounted with such mischief in her eyes at the memory that he just knew it was all still bubbling up inside her.

He took her home after the meal, and she turned at the door and flashed him that wonderful megawatt smile of hers. 'It's a tip inside,' she confessed, 'but you're welcome to come in.'

It was a tip. It was more of a tip than she'd realised, because her flatmate had decided to have a party and it was littered with people hell-bent on enjoying themselves.

'Ah,' she said, having found that even her room had been taken over and there was no escape.

'Come back to mine,' he suggested, wondering how he could be noble and not make love to her once he'd got her alone in his apartment. They walked through the door, and he deliberately didn't reach for the switch so that she could see London stretched out below them, a million sparkling lights reaching out to the horizon.

'Oh, wow,' she said, and laughed a little breathlessly. 'That's so pretty. London at its best—you can't see it.'

He chuckled and moved to stand behind her, aching to take her in his arms. He could smell her perfume, feel the warmth radiating off her. He dragged his eyes from the delicate, creamy nape of her neck and back to the view reluctantly. Not so reluctantly. He loved it. It put everything else in perspective. Even his longing for her.

'It's beautiful,' he said quietly. 'Sometimes I sit here for hours in the dark and just stare out over it—recharge the batteries.'

She turned, looking up at him with eyes that were serious for once. 'You have trouble with that, don't you? Recharging your batteries? You ought to do more fun things—go to the zoo, go to the park—anything, really. You need to learn how to relax.'

He smiled a little sadly. 'With you?' he murmured. 'You're the least relaxing person I know.'

'I don't have to be. I can be quiet—I often am. It's only with you I'm like this—so alive.'

Odd, how she'd echoed his thoughts, as if it was only when they were together that they became whole.

'You're beautiful,' he said without stopping to think. 'I want to make love to you, Laurie.'

Her smile was gentle and full of promise. 'Good,' she whispered.

He closed his eyes and counted to ten. He was going to die. His heart was going to stop, or rupture or something. Either that or it was a dream. He opened his eyes and she was still there, her smile tentative, and his heart was still beating.

'You're so lovely,' he whispered, his thumb coming up to trace her cheekbone, the angle of her jaw, the soft, rosy fullness of her lips. The skin dragged a little and the tip of her tongue flicked out to touch his thumb, moistening its path. It was unbearably erotic, and a groan erupted from deep in his throat.

Her hands slid up his chest, over his shoulders, tunnelling through his hair and drawing him down. Their lips met, coaxing, sipping, teasing, and then something seemed to shift, some elemental force within them that rose up and took over, and they were both consumed in a primitive fire that swept everything in its path.

As the fire died away and left just the ashes of their passion, they found they were in the bedroom, with no clear idea of how they'd got there. He imagined they must have walked, or maybe he'd carried her, or dragged her by her hair. Nothing would have surprised him.

He touched her face with fingers that trembled. 'Wow,' he said softly, his voice ragged. 'That was—'

'Amazing,' she said huskily and, leaning towards him, she pressed her lips lightly to his. 'It was the most beautiful thing.'

He laughed a little unsteadily. 'You see, we can agree on something,' he teased, and she smiled and kissed him again—and again—and again.

It was the start of a personal life as wild and tempestuous as their working life, and even more satisfying. Within weeks they were married, and the next three or four years had been bliss.

And now, he thought heavily, all that wonderful humour and sparkle seemed to have gone and, far from arguing with him, she didn't even want to talk. She just wanted to run.

And cry. That was the awful bit, seeing her cry. He'd hardly ever seen her cry, and never without him.

A lump rose in his throat, and he swallowed it. Oh, Laurie, where did we go wrong? he asked himself. When did you stop answering back and fighting me? And why? You've never been afraid to tell me in the past if you didn't like something. Why now?

He needed to move. His neck was at an awkward angle, but he didn't want to get up without giving her time to compose herself and wash her face. He grunted and shifted his legs, watching her through eyes open just the merest fraction, and she came awake with a little start, sat up and scrubbed her cheeks, then with the dog at her heels, she tiptoed out of the room, closing the door behind her with a soft click.

Rob sighed and stood up and rolled his head, arching his back and stretching his arms above his head. They hit the low ceiling, and he looked around, studying the room for the first time.

It was comfortable—nothing special, but the atmosphere was cosy. He thought of their home in London, and wished they had a room as cosy as this to curl up in. But when? There was never time. He could hardly remember the colour of the walls, never mind the last time he'd sat down long enough to fall asleep.

He threw some more coal on the fire and prodded it into life, and it crackled and spat, little flames licking up around the new coals. He held out his hands to it, rubbing them together. There was something primitively satisfying about a real fire. They should have one at home more often—if they still had a home together, that was.

He refused to admit defeat. And at least now, having seen her cry, he knew she wasn't indifferent to him. That might have been impossible to overcome.

He could hear her moving around in the bathroom next door, then the kitchen, and a few minutes later she reappeared with another tray of tea.

'Hi,' she said, smiling brightly, but it didn't reach her eyes. 'I made tea earlier but you were sleeping. I've done some fresh.'

'You should have woken me when you made the first lot,' he said, and he thought her shoulders squared a fraction. Because she thought it was a criticism? Oh, hell.

'You looked tired,' she said, sounding defensive. 'I thought I'd just leave you. I knew you'd wake up soon, you always do. Here—and there's some cake, if you like. I don't know what it's like, I bought it at the local shop yesterday.'

'I'm sure it'll be fine. I hope you got plenty of food in while you were there—or should we save it?'

She shook her head. 'I bought quite a bit. Enough for a few days, anyway. I don't think we need to start rationing ourselves.'

'Let's hope it stops snowing, then. I don't fancy starving to death if we're stuck here for too long.'

For a moment her face reflected panic—at the thought of being shut up with him? Not so very long ago they would have revelled in it.

Not that he could afford to be out of circulation for long, whatever happened. He was expected back in New York on Monday, and it was Friday evening now.

She looked out of the window, shivering slightly as the gale squeezed round the frame and cooled the air several degrees. She pulled the curtain shut again and her chin went up a notch defiantly. 'I'm sure we won't be stranded long—this is Scotland, after all. They're used to it. They'll have snow ploughs out in the night—I expect it'll be clear by the morning.'

'We could always eat the dog,' he said, to lighten the mood, but she just glared at him.

'It's not funny—and anyway, I have to work.'

'You can work. So long as the power's on, you can work—and so, I suppose, can I. I should check my email.'

He slid his mobile phone out of his pocket and looked at it in disgust. 'There's no signal!'

'No. I know. You'll have to use my desktop—if I'm feeling generous.'

He snorted. 'I've got to get to it first, and frankly, just at the moment, I don't fancy it.'

'You could have a bit of string,' she suggested. 'Like they have going down potholes and things, so they can find the way back.' Her mouth was twitching ever so slightly, and he grunted.

'That's not such a stupid idea. It isn't funny out there. I seriously thought I wasn't going to find the cottage again. Let's face it, neither of us knows the lie of the land. You've only been here a few hours longer than I have. I suggest we leave it till the morning and see how it is then. Nothing can be that important.'

In fact there were several things eating at the fringes of his conscience, but he wasn't risking his life to deal with it. He'd probably just lose a whole pile of money from not shuffling it in time, but it was almost close of business in New York, and nothing would happen until Monday morning. Maybe he could rescue the situation then. If not, tough. You win some, you lose some, he reminded himself.

And not losing Laurie was much more important than the price of a few stocks and shares.

She turned on the television and found a local news channel. It did nothing to inspire confidence in the weather, he thought. She stared at the forecast, her face dismayed, and he hoped that the few provisions she'd got in the day before really would be enough to see them through, because he had a feeling they would be there longer than either of them imagined.

'Supper?' she said brightly, flicking the television off again and turning to him with a tense little smile.

'That would be good. Let me give you a hand.'

'There's no need,' she said, heading for the door with the tea tray, but he was right behind her, the dog tagging along to referee. He didn't intend to waste a moment of their time together sitting in another room while she stomped round the kitchen resenting the fact that she was having to cook for him!

Oh, no. She had enough ammunition already, he realised dimly. He was damned if he was giving her any more!

He would insist on following her. She wanted to go into the kitchen alone and assimilate the knowledge that they were genuinely going to be stuck together for ages, so she could gird her loins, so to speak, and work out a game plan.

Not that there was any point. Rob would just quietly do the other thing, so she might as well save her breath.

He took the tray from her and washed up the mugs and plates, and she stood for a moment and stared at the unaccustomed sight of him with his hands in the sink.

Good grief! Pity she didn't have a camera.

'So, what are we having?' he asked, and Laurie sighed and opened the fridge.

'Pasta and tomato bake?'

He gave her a look that just might have been horror over his shoulder. 'Really?'

'Really. What's the matter—no meat? There's a tin of dog food if you're desperate. I don't eat meat any more.'

He looked even more horrified. 'You don't?'

'No. I don't. I haven't done for months—only the odd bit of chicken or fish very occasionally.' And it said a lot about the state of their relationship that he hadn't even noticed—hadn't been there to notice.

She turned the oven on and found a likely dish while he stood propped up against the front of the sink, only slightly in the way, and watched her as she mixed the pasta and the jar of sauce together, grated cheese on top and put it in the oven. Then they had half an hour to kill. She put the kettle on and thought fast.

'I think there's some bedding in the cupboard on the landing,' she told him. 'A quilt of some sort. You can use that. We'll sort you out while it cooks.'

She went upstairs, Rob on her heels, and found the quilt in the cupboard. It was a bit thin, but he'd got the fire as well as the central heating. She held it up. It wasn't very long, either, but then nor was the sofa.

He'd live, she told herself, refusing to weaken, and thrust the things at him. 'Here—there's a pillow, too. That do you?'

He arched an eloquent brow and turned and went

downstairs, dropping the things onto the sofa before following her back into the kitchen without a word. The room seemed to shrink as he arrived back in it, his presence as much as his size dwarfing it and crowding her aura.

She took refuge on the far side of the table, sitting down out of the way while the kettle boiled.

'Tea or coffee?' he asked as it clicked.

She looked at him in astonishment. 'Coffee, please. Black, no sugar.'

'I know how you take your coffee—unless it's changed, like everything else.'

'Nothing else has changed,' she said defensively.

'Except you're vegetarian now, and you seem to be living in Scotland.'

There was no answer to that, so she didn't bother. She waited, instead, for the coffee that he set in front of her, then busied herself drinking it, giving it far more attention than a simple beverage could possibly warrant.

He said nothing, just waited her out again, and in the end she jumped up and found some plates and put them in the top oven to warm. She opened the door of the lower oven to check on the pasta, and a wonderful waft of rich tomato drifted out.

'It smells good,' he said, breaking the silence.

'Surprise, surprise.'

'I am surprised. It also smells a little familiar. I suppose it's one of the things you've been feeding me that I thought you'd spent hours cooking.'

She felt heat climb her cheeks. 'I have used it a few times,' she confessed. 'With tuna or chicken in it. I stir fresh cream into it and chop herbs over the top sometimes instead of the cheese. That gives it a more luxury feel as opposed to the home-grown rustic gratin.' Her smile was wry. 'It's quite versatile.'

He shook his head slowly, a rueful chuckle rumbling in his chest. 'Clever—but then you always were. I should have realised you wouldn't be content to twiddle your thumbs in between domestic chores.'

'You were never at home to notice what I was doing,' she said with a shrug. 'Why should you think about it?'

'Because, like it or not, I'm your husband?' he said softly, and she retreated behind the table again and played with the dregs of her cold coffee. She wasn't ready to start this conversation—not until she knew how she felt, and had all her emotional ducks in a row.

Rob, however, wasn't content to leave it alone. Why did she imagine he would be? 'I should have known what you were doing,' he went on, watching her thoughtfully from his position on the other side of the table. 'It rather shocks me that for a year, either you've been lying about what you've done all day, or I've simply failed to ask.'

She coloured again. 'Both,' she said honestly. 'When you did ask, I didn't so much lie as be frugal with the truth.'

He snorted, getting up to dump his mug in the sink and rinse it out. He turned to reach for hers just as she stood up, and they collided.

She all but leapt back out of his way. Crazy. How long had they been together? Years. And how many times had they accidentally bumped into each other? And yet now, today, it sent electric sparks shooting through her body and left her knees bereft of strength.

She checked the pasta again, poking it to see if the little tubes were tender. They were. Thank God for that.

It meant they could eat, and when they'd eaten, they could go to bed—separately!—and she could have a few hours of peace and quiet to gather her jumbled emotions.

She set the dish down on a mat on the table, rummaged around for cutlery and pulled the plates out of the top oven.

'I don't suppose you've got a nice bottle of some Italian red tucked away anywhere?' he said hopefully, but she didn't reply. She did, in fact, have a bottle of wine tucked away in a cupboard, but she wasn't getting it out now, either for him or herself.

She needed all her faculties about her, because she knew, as bedtime drew closer, he was going to pile on the charm and try and coax his way into her bed. So, no wine, even if she felt inclined, which she didn't.

'There's water in the tap,' she said, sounding like her grandmother, and he chuckled softly and filled two glasses, setting them down on the table and pulling out his chair.

'Let's eat, then. I'm starving.'

Thank goodness she'd chucked in another couple of handfuls of pasta and a little extra water! She gave him the lion's share, but he still cleaned his plate before she'd finished, and looked around hopefully.

Heavens. She'd forgotten how much he could eat. She cast a mental eye over her provisions and wondered if, indeed, they did have enough food if they were cut off for long. One thing was sure, they were going to get through it a lot more than twice as fast!

'There's a tin of rice pudding,' she offered, and he wrinkled his nose.

'I prefer your homemade version,' he confessed, and

then cocked an eyebrow at her as she shifted uncomfortably. 'I suppose the real coffee's instant as well.'

She gave an awkward laugh. 'No, the real coffee's real.'

He sighed with relief. 'Thank God for small mercies,' he said under his breath, and she stifled a chuckle.

She heated the rice pudding, put it under the grill for a moment to skin over and brown, then dished it up. 'Just like mother used to make,' she said with a wry grin, and he looked up at her with a smile in his eyes that nearly melted her bones.

Don't, she thought, plonking his bowl down in front of him. Please don't turn on the charm.

She scraped the dish out into her bowl, sat down and ate without looking at him again. God forbid she should catch those gorgeous cobalt blue eyes again. She'd be lost.

They cleared up the kitchen together, and then he went out into the teeth of the gale and brought in the bag of coal from the little bunker at the end of the cottage.

'Is this all you've got?' he asked, and she nodded.

'I found it here. It's that and the half-tank of heating oil—oh, and there's an electric fire on the landing we could use, but it's very expensive.'

'I think I can probably afford a little electricity,' he said drily, and she bristled.

'My bill—my house, remember?'

'How could I forget?' he muttered under his breath, and banked up the fire ready for the night.

She hovered in the doorway. 'Right, I'll say good-night. You can have the bathroom after me.'

'You're so kind.'

She ignored that, closing the door softly behind her with a little click and beating a hasty retreat. Better the sarcasm than the charm, she thought with a slight smile. She could resist the sarcasm!

But there was a tiny bit of her—a bit she refused to acknowledge—that was disappointed he hadn't tried just a little harder to convince her to let him share her bed…

CHAPTER FOUR

IT WAS freezing upstairs. The wind seemed to shriek through the little dormer window, and Laurie huddled under the super-warm quilt and shivered.

Of course if it hadn't been for her stupid pride she could have been snuggled up in bed with Rob, just as they had been for the last five years, so she had only herself to blame if she froze to death.

Socks. Socks and tracksuit bottoms—and a fleece. She rummaged in the drawers, dragged the extra clothes on and shot back into bed, pulling the covers over her head. It was still freezing. In fact, she thought, a while later, it was getting colder and colder. Perhaps she'd try the electric fire as well.

She got up and turned on the light, but nothing happened. Funny, it was all right a little while ago. A little frown pleating her brow, she flicked the switch again, then the landing light switch outside the door, but there was nothing.

Not the power, she thought with a tiny inward wail of despair. Please, not the power. Not now, tonight, of all nights, when the only source of heat, other than the boiler with its electric programmer and pump, was downstairs in the same room as Rob and the faithless dog.

So she couldn't even cuddle up to Midas, because he'd sneaked in there while she was in the bathroom and was last seen making himself at home on the chair by the fire, with Rob's active encouragement. She got back into bed, leaving the door open to allow any escaping heat from the sitting room to drift in, but the wind round the front door seemed to find the way to her bones faster than any slight trace of warmth, and she got up and closed it again.

Odd, how lonely and isolated she felt with the two of them downstairs warm and comfortable while she froze senseless up here alone. Senseless being the operative word, of course, because there was nothing to stop her taking her quilt and going downstairs to the chair. Or the settee, come to that. After all, who was paying the rent?

Rob could have the chair—and Midas could manage to sleep on the floor. He usually did, without a murmur—but then he wasn't usually encouraged to flout the rules quite so indulgently.

She sniffed in disgust. Her nose was running with the cold, and her hands and feet were like ice, but sheer pride kept her rooted shivering in the bed until almost four, when she was so cold and so wretched she gave in and crept downstairs, groping her way in the dark.

She opened the door to the sitting room and the warmth hit her like a tidal wave. Bliss. She must have been mad to wait so long, she thought with a shiver. Midas thumped his tail, and between the noise and the slight glow from the fire, she found her way to the chair and evicted the guilty but reluctant dog. He'd warmed it beautifully, of course. She curled up in it after she'd put a little more coal on the fire, and huddled under the quilt, her feet tucked under her bottom and her head resting on the arm.

Midas lay on the bottom of the quilt, which was a

nuisance in a way because he tugged it down a little and her neck was in a slight draught, but it was nothing compared to the cold upstairs and she didn't have the heart to throw him off that, too.

Gradually she started to thaw and relax, revelling in the glorious warmth. All she had to do was wake up early enough to remove the evidence and get out of there before Rob woke at eight or so. At least with his jet lag he was likely to sleep in a bit, and he hadn't stirred so much as an eyelash while she'd been settling in.

Thank goodness. At least she wouldn't have to tolerate the merciless ribbing about giving in and seeking out his company!

Comforted by the thought and the warmth, within a few minutes she drifted off to sleep.

Rob lay quietly listening to the soft, even sound of her breathing. He didn't know why she'd come down, but he couldn't hear the boiler running and guessed the power might be off. There was absolute blackness in the cottage, not a trace of light from anywhere, and that and the silence was a pretty sure sign.

That meant, of course, that as well as the boiler they'd have no kettle, no TV or radio, no computer, no email or fax, no cooker—just a few shovelfuls of coal between them and hypothermia. And, in the interests of preserving fuel, they would have to share their body heat.

A slow smile played over his lips in the darkness, and he shifted to his side, trying not to focus too firmly on the accompanying benefits. Assuming he could talk her into it, of course—although knowing his luck, the power would be on again by morning anyway.

Still, a man could always hope...

* * *

She overslept. The first inkling of wakefulness came in response to a soft rattle and a hiss coming from the fire.

Damn, she thought, her heart sinking. He's awake.

She listened to what was obviously the sound of water coming to the boil, then the slopping, pouring noise of it being decanted out into a mug—twice, which meant one of the mugs of tea was destined for her.

Crunch time.

She opened one eye cautiously and found Rob crouched on the hearthrug staring straight at her, his face unreadable in the half-light from the partly opened curtains.

'Tea's up,' he said softly. 'The power's still off. Where's the cold water tank? We don't want it to freeze.'

She shrugged. 'I don't know. It must be in the little bedroom over here. I don't have a key for it, though.'

'Just so long as it *is* over this room,' he said thoughtfully. 'It's so cold outside the pipes'll freeze without warmth, but the ceiling probably lets through a good bit. Let's just hope we don't run out of coal before the heating's back on.'

The idea was unthinkable, and she shuddered.

'Don't panic,' he said with a slightly cocky smile. 'I can keep you warm.'

She didn't attempt to hide the snort, and he grinned and shrugged. 'Ah, well, it was worth a try. Anyway, if we run out of coal, I'll have to go and get some.'

'What, you're going to walk over the mountain and carry it back over your shoulder? Don't be a hero,' she said disgustedly. 'You'll just die—and anyway, even if you could walk that far, you could only carry enough to last a day. We'd do better to burn the kitchen table.'

'I'd like to see you explain that one to the owners,' he said drily. 'I don't suppose the fire clause in their insurance covers arson. However, what I was thinking,' he went on in a mild voice that made her want to scream, 'is that the local farmers have tractors that could probably get through most of it. If we could persuade them to take me to the nearest coal merchants—'

She laughed. 'You do realise where you are, don't you? They don't have coal merchants in this part of Scotland like they do in the towns. They sell peat in little bags in the caravan shop, or they get it delivered by the ton from ten or so miles away. Anyway, I don't know any local farmers, and I doubt if they realise there's anyone here, even assuming they had a benign fit towards us, and why should they? We're newcomers—foreigners.'

'Ah, but we're Fergusons. They might be fooled. And little bags of peat from the caravan shop would do fine—or maybe I could persuade a farmer to flog us a few logs.'

Unlikely. There had been precious little sign of any local farmers since she'd moved, but she'd only been there twenty-four hours before the snow fell, so it was probably quite early days. Maybe he was right. What a sickening thought.

She shot him a baleful glare and wondered how she managed to feel so foul. She was usually sunny in the morning. It must be lack of sleep and being wretched with cold. Whatever, she couldn't be bothered to be nice and, having been taught that if you didn't have anything nice to say you shouldn't say anything at all, she buttoned her lip and concentrated on sipping the tea he put into her hand.

Her fingers curled gratefully round the warmth and settled with relief, and she wriggled up into more of a sitting position. Instantly the muscles of her right calf coiled up in a tight ball and gave her hell. She tried not to let the little scream of pain past her lips. It would ease in a moment—surely—

'What is it?'

'Cramp,' she bit out, slopping the tea in the effort to put it down and stretch out her leg.

He was there before her, twitching aside the quilt, one big, firm hand grasping her calf and stretching and pulling the muscle out as his other hand pressed firmly up on her toes, easing out the knot. He was kneeling in front of her, her heel resting on the firm, solid warmth of his thigh while he worked. It felt wonderful, not least because his hands were on her and she needed that—needed him, if the truth be told, but only on her terms. Not just any terms—and certainly not the old ones.

She felt the knot give, relaxing under the exquisitely painful onslaught of his clever fingers, and she sighed with relief.

'Better?' he asked, sitting back, and she nodded, pulling her foot away from him and suppressing the little pang of regret that the contact between them was broken. It was better this way—safer. She tucked her legs back up under her and pulled the quilt over them again before she gave into the urge to stay there, resting the soles of her feet on his thighs and absorbing their glorious and very tempting warmth.

He gave her an unreadable look and retreated into the corner of the settee, making himself comfortable and coincidentally getting rather a long way from her. He picked up his tea again and studied it thoughtfully, and for some irrational reason she felt shut out.

She wished she knew what was going through his head, but she had a funny feeling she'd rather not know. So far he'd left the subject of her escape from London pretty much alone, but she had an idea that that state of affairs was shortly coming to an end. He looked as if he was warming up to say something, and she didn't think she'd like it.

Finally he broke the silence, but not in the way she'd expected at all, and she almost laughed with relief.

'If you want to have a bath,' he said, 'it would be an idea to do it while the tank's still got any hot water in it. You might as well use it up.'

What a wonderful idea—except that it was impossible. 'No tank,' she explained regretfully, thinking with longing of a slow, lazy bubblebath in the jacuzzi at home. 'It's a combination boiler—it gives instant hot water without storing it. More fuel efficient, so the agent said. She was very proud of that.'

Rob snorted. 'Oh, well, there are always cold showers,' he said with a vain attempt at humour, and she laughed. There was a slightly hysterical edge to it, and she cut it off abruptly.

'Rather more your department than mine, I think?' she said drily.

He just arched a brow at her and returned his attention to the tea. She noticed, for the first time, that he'd brought a saucepan in and must have nestled it in the coals to boil the water. Good idea. At least they could still cook, after a fashion, even if it was only fried or boiled.

Sounds like eggs, she thought, and suppressed another

hysterical laugh. Tea and eggs—and then she wondered if she'd got enough milk. She didn't use it in coffee, so she probably wouldn't have bought much. Rob, on the other hand, took it in both tea and coffee, and couldn't stand either of them black.

Tough. It was an emergency, after all, and it wasn't as if he'd been invited. He could rough it.

'I wonder how long the power's going to be off,' she murmured, thinking aloud. 'I ought to be working.'

He laughed. 'Got a shovel?'

'Shovel?'

He pulled the curtain open further, and she sat forwards and looked out into a featureless white wilderness. The garage had disappeared, only one end of the gable sticking out of the huge white mound that seemed to be the drive. Of the cars there was no sign, not so much as the merest hump in the snow.

'Ah,' she said, and dredged up a smile. 'The shovel would be in the garage.'

He gave a strangled laugh. 'I thought as much. Oh, well, I dare say the world can live without us. Shall I boil some water for washing?'

'More tea would slip down a treat,' she suggested, pushing her luck, but he simply smiled.

'Why not? We don't have to rush to the office.'

'Talking of rushing, I don't suppose there's any way we can let the dog out?'

Their eyes tracked in unison to Midas, whining hopefully at the door, his tail wafting gently from side to side.

'Hmm. Well, I can try. Got an oven tray or something like that? I can use it to scoop some of the snow off the path—unless you've got a better idea?'

She shook her head. It had occurred to her to let him out of the window, but then the dog would be into snow over his head and wouldn't be able to get back inside. No, an oven tray sounded wonderful—or better still, the grill pan, if it had a fixed handle.

She stood up, unravelling her legs from the quilt, and headed for the kitchen, shivering at the sudden blast of cold outside the cosy little room. The estate agent's words came back to her—'It won't be very expensive, that far north.'

How far? Try the Arctic, she thought, the hysteria rising again. She quelled it ruthlessly. Really, she was about to lose it. She rummaged around in the kitchen and found the grill pan—the fixed handle sort, miraculously—and took it back to him, then braved a visit to the bathroom.

She thought she was going to freeze to the loo seat for a moment, and vowed to block up the cat flap in the wall that let in a howling gale. Fair enough in the summer, she thought, but now! She'd find an old newspaper and stuff it with that. Although the draught did seem to have got much worse in the last few seconds...

She emerged to find the front door open and Rob busy shovelling snow out of the hall.

'Oops,' she said cautiously, and he shot her a baleful look over his shoulder.

'It fell in when I opened the door. The wind must be from a very unusual direction, because these old places were built usually with their backs to the wind just so this didn't happen.'

'Take it up with the architect,' she advised drily, and peered past him. 'Where's the dog?'

'Bouncing around. He's got no choice—if he doesn't

bounce, he can't move. He'll be in in a minute, I expect. Not even Midas will be out long in this.'

He picked up the mat, shook it off round the corner of the door without setting foot outside, then closed the door against the wind.

'Hell's teeth, it's cold out there. I think I'll have a cup of tea and pull some more clothes on before I go looking for the shovel—if I even bother. Maybe we'll manage with the grill pan for now.'

There was a scratching at the door, and he opened it to let Midas in, but the dog whined and bounced away again, back over his tracks, and began digging furiously.

Rob sighed shortly 'What on earth is he up to? Midas? Come here before we freeze to death.'

The dog ignored him, and Laurie peered past him to see what he was up to. He certainly seemed like a dog with a mission. 'It looks as though he's found something.'

'Well, he can stay out there another minute while I get dressed in something thicker,' Rob said, and shut the door emphatically.

Laurie went back into the sitting room with him, hovering by the window so she could watch Midas and see what he was up to while Rob rummaged in his suitcase and pulled on extra clothes.

'He's definitely found something—look! He's digging furiously and sniffing and I can hear him whining even from this distance. What on earth can it be?'

'It's probably a frozen rabbit.'

'I don't think they have rabbits round here. Too cold and wet.'

'A deer?'

'Maybe,' she said doubtfully, and carried on watching.

'I don't suppose you'd like to get your coat on and come out there with me?' Rob said drily.

She smiled. 'Oh, I thought I'd let you do the heroic, manly thing. I'd hate to steal your thunder.'

He snorted in disgust and headed for the door, his coat buttoned up to his neck and a poloneck sweater pulled up over his ears under the upturned collar.

She looked down at his feet. 'Um—no boots?'

He glowered darkly. 'Oh, yes, I've got boots—in the car. There was only so much I could carry last night. I'll go and get them, shall I?'

'Good idea.'

She controlled the smirk—just—and ran upstairs and pulled her clothes on quickly once he'd left the cottage. They were freezing, of course, but pride forbade her to slob about in the tracksuit bottoms over her nightshirt! Anyway, she'd soon warm up. She ran back down to the warm sitting room and hovered between the window and the fire, watching.

He'd reached the dog by wading through snow drifts, and now he was scraping away with the grill pan. Suddenly he stopped, and dropping the grill pan, he started to use his bare hands, scraping the snow carefully away from whatever he'd found.

Midas was almost beside himself, bouncing and barking and whining and rushing backwards and forwards, sniffing whatever it was before digging furiously again beside Rob. What on earth was it? For a moment she regretted not going out there, but then all rational thought fled as Rob straightened with something black and woolly in his arms.

A sheep? No—a lamb?

Or—a dog?

She ran to the door and opened it just as Rob reached it, bearing his burden with huge care and tenderness.

'It's a collie!' she exclaimed. 'Oh, my goodness—is it alive?'

'I think so—it's very cold, but I think it must be alive because it's not stiff. It must have been there hours, but the snow covering must have protected it from the wind. We need to get it into the warm.'

She shut the front door behind him and the demented Midas, and led them through into the sitting room, making a space by the fire.

'No—the chair. The floor will be too draughty and too near the fire at first. We'll have to do this slowly.'

So she stripped the quilt off the chair and pushed it towards the hearth, got a blanket from the dog's bed in the kitchen and spread it out on the chair, and Rob gently laid the poor dog down on it.

Feeble as it was, a pink tongue came out and licked his hand, and his face crumpled slightly.

'Ah, hell,' he said, turning his head so Laurie couldn't see, but it was too late, and she felt her heart contract. She'd forgotten this side of him, the tender side that couldn't bear suffering. It was so long since she'd seen it, that was why.

His hand stroked its head gently, his fingers coming away damp from the sodden fur. 'Poor old thing,' he murmured, his voice gruff. 'It's as thin as a rake—it must be a stray. No farm dog would be this thin, it couldn't manage to work.'

'I'll get some water for it—is it a dog or a bitch?'

'I don't know—a bitch, I think. Yes. Oh, poor baby.' He stroked the shivering dog with his gentle hand, and she licked it again, just once, before collapsing back against the chair arm.

'Warm water,' Laurie murmured, pouring the water they'd heated for their tea into the fresh cold water in the dog's bowl. She just hoped Midas didn't mind the interloper borrowing his blanket and his bowl, but he didn't seem to, he seemed much more interested in licking her all over, his rough tongue lashing across her body over and over again, her head and face, her ears, her shoulder, her feet—anything he could reach.

And gradually, as he licked and licked, she seemed to come round a bit, as if the massage from his tongue was warming her cold, stiff body and bringing it back to life. She lifted her head and licked at Midas weakly, and he turned his head back to hers and licked her face again.

The curiously tender gesture brought a lump to Laurie's throat, and she had to swallow hard.

'I think we can leave him to it,' Rob said softly. 'He seems to know what to do. How about making us another cup of tea while I retrieve the grill pan?'

She nodded, refilled their impromptu kettle in a quick sortie to the kitchen and went back, pan in one hand, bread and butter in the other just as he came in through the door.

'Breakfast?' she suggested, holding up the loaf, and he arched a brow.

'What happened to the full English?' he murmured, but she ignored him.

'We can make toast over the fire.'

'Only if you're prepared to hold it,' he said with a short laugh.

'Oh, ye of little faith.' She produced a toasting fork from the hearth behind the companion set, and after settling the saucepan of water on the fire in a little dip in the coals, she carefully speared a slice of bread and held it over the heat.

'Smoked bread—oh, yeah,' Rob murmured, but she turned it over and it was golden brown. He fell silent, and when it was done he reached out his hand and she removed the toast and put the fork in his hand.

He took it, a quizzical look on his face. 'Not quite what I had in mind. I thought, as I'd done all the heroic digging-in-the-snow stuff, you might want to feed me.'

But there was a teasing light in his eyes as he speared his own bread and toasted it, settling down beside her on the floor in front of the hearth. She relented enough to make two cups of tea and handed one to him, stunned to feel how cold his hands still were. She instantly felt guilty, and had to remind herself that he was thirty-one years old and quite capable of taking care of himself.

He should have had gloves on, she thought, doing her grandmother impressions again, but his only gloves were soft kid leather and probably wouldn't have helped much anyway. You'd need sheepskin to keep that lot out.

She settled back against the front of the sofa and watched Midas with the little collie. Having licked all he could reach from the ground, he was now standing over her, nosing her out of the way, then licking the other side as she shifted.

Then, with a grunting sigh, he settled down behind her and curled his big, warm body round her. Laurie was worried he'd squash the life out of her, but apparently not.

Still shuddering occasionally, she tucked her nose into her paws and went to sleep.

'I wonder what the owners would make of our use of

their furniture,' Laurie murmured. 'Although they didn't mind pets, the agent said, and there's a cat flap in the bathroom wall.'

'I noticed,' he said drily. 'I thought I'd stuff a cushion in it.'

'I thought newspaper—it won't matter if it leaks, then.'

'Good idea. Whatever, it needs stuffing. It's freezing in there.'

'It was nice with the heating,' she said, oddly defensive. 'It's only because the power's off.'

He gave her an odd look. 'I do realise that,' he said gently, and she felt an idiot. What a silly thing to be arguing about.

Well, not really arguing, exactly, but—

'More tea?'

She nodded. 'Please.'

'I'll brave the kitchen and get water. You can make more toast.'

And with that he unfolded himself from the floor and went out, Midas watching him with one eye.

'You're a good boy,' she said softly, and he thumped his tail. He looked pleased with himself, as well he might. Laurie thought how awful she would have felt if the snow had thawed and she'd found the body of his little friend frozen under a bush—especially if she'd called him in and insisted he came.

Although, looking at his obvious devotion to his new companion, maybe he would simply have refused to obey her. She wondered how devoted he'd be when it came to sharing his food—although she'd brought a big bag of his dried food from home, so they weren't likely to run out—at least, not before she'd starved to death. He had many more days' supply than she did!

She found herself wondering idly what dog food tasted like as she browned a couple more slices of her dwindling bread supply over the fire. Maybe they'd find out, but she hoped not. After all, the snow had stopped falling, and it looked almost civilised out there now, if a little cold.

And even having to be locked up with Rob wasn't proving too arduous, she realised with surprise. They seemed to have brokered an unspoken truce—agreed to disagree or somesuch. Amazing. Maybe if they continued to avoid the subject they'd survive the experience without killing each other.

He came back in, and she retreated to one corner of the settee while he put the pan on the fire to heat. It seemed to take ages, and the silence seemed to grow tighter and tighter. Was it her imagination?

Or her guilty conscience?

She didn't need to have a guilty conscience, she reminded herself while she munched her piece of toast. She was a free woman, not a slave. Nevertheless, she did feel guilty—and it annoyed the heck out of her.

He handed her her tea, sat back into the other corner of the settee and gave her a level look over the top of his mug.

'The dogs seem fine,' she said quickly. 'She's stopped shivering. I wonder what she's called? She hasn't got a collar on.'

'She's probably a stray.'

'Poor thing. You've got toast there, by the way.'

He just looked at her, that level, searching look that made her heart sink.

'Stop procrastinating,' he said in a voice that brooked no argument. 'I think it's time we had a little chat, don't you? Suppose you tell me what this is all about—why you ran away.'

'I didn't run—'

'No, you drove—in a car you'd bought yourself, with income from a company you're running that I didn't even know about. I think I deserve an explanation, Laurie, and I'm not moving until I get one.'

So much for their truce!

CHAPTER FIVE

'LET'S start with why,' he said, his voice slightly softer, and it made her want to cry.

She swallowed hard. No way was she giving him the satisfaction of seeing her cry, but she owed him her honesty.

'I just felt trapped,' she said slowly. 'I felt we'd lost our sparkle. I didn't know you any more, you were never there, and when you were all we seemed to do was try and get me pregnant.'

'Is that the trouble? Is it because you can't conceive? Or because you don't want to?' He hesitated, and his eyes speared her like twin blue lasers. 'Tell me something, Laurie—are you on the Pill?'

She stared at him, shocked. 'On the Pill? Don't be so silly. Why should I be on the Pill?'

He shrugged. 'I don't know. You tell me. So you don't get pregnant?' He looked away, his face taut, and when he next spoke his voice was quiet and deathly with control. 'Are you having an affair, Laurie? Is that it?'

She nearly dropped her mug. Instead she set it down, very carefully, and wrapped her arms round her knees. He thought that? He really thought she'd do that?

'I can't believe you think I'd do that,' she said hollowly. 'Why would I do that?'

'Because you're bored? Because I'm never there? Because all you want is my money, and my constant absence is actually a bonus, only now, of course, you don't need the money—'

'Stop! Rob, that's just not true! I wouldn't do that!' She was hurt, rubbed raw by the doubt in his voice and his bitter accusations, despite the fact that she had given him plenty of reasons to ask such questions. But even so, how could he not know her better than that? 'I couldn't do it,' she went on, shaking her head slowly in disbelief. 'I wouldn't have an *affair!* Sex isn't that important—'

'Isn't it? It used to be—for both of us.'

His eyes locked with hers, burning like blue flames, the heat scorching her. She remembered when they'd been eager lovers, unable to get enough of each other, their hands and mouths greedy, their bodies insatiable. Heat pooled in her and she looked hastily away.

How long ago it seemed—and what a sad and lonely road she'd trodden since.

'Anyway, I didn't say anything about sex,' he went on. 'You might have met someone else and fallen in love. Someone who had time for you—who was there when I couldn't be.' His voice was taut, but she didn't really hear the pain in it, only the words.

Someone who was there. Someone who actually noticed her. What a thought. 'It sounds tempting,' she said a little bitterly. 'And you're right, I was alone too much. So much so that I thought, if I was going to be alone, I might just as well do it properly and really be alone—hence the move. Although I must say it doesn't really feel very different, except for the location. I haven't been any more alone here than I was in Hertfordshire, or it hasn't felt like it. I'm amazed you missed me, but then I suppose if I rolled up the carpet in the hall, you might realise something was missing. I'm just an extension of the furniture, something that's always there. Sometimes I don't think you even know I'm alive,' she said sadly, and he gave a short, humourless huff of laughter.

'Oh, Laurie, don't be stupid. Of course I know you're alive. I think about you all the time.'

'No, you don't,' she said bluntly. 'You don't think about anything but work, even when you're at home. You're totally focused.'

'That doesn't mean I don't think about you on another plane.'

'But you don't know what I'm doing. You're quite unaware of my activities. You're never there to know what I'm doing.'

'And you chose not to tell me,' he pointed out, his voice hardening again. 'You know where I am—you can ring me at any time and talk to me—I tell you what I'm doing every minute of every day. You don't tell me anything—or at least, not the truth.'

'I was going to.' Her conscience was troubling her on that, and had almost since the beginning, but it had just never seemed to be the right time, and after a while it had grown even harder to know how to tell him. Now it was too late for anything but damage limitation.

She sighed harshly and scrubbed her hands over her face. 'I didn't keep it a secret so you wouldn't know,' she said, trying to explain. 'I just didn't want to tell you at first because I thought you'd laugh or shoot it down in flames or tell me I was doing it wrong and take over—'

'As if you've never done that to me.'

She remembered their wrangles at work, and coloured slightly. 'I know. You must have hated it.'

'Not as much as I hated it when it stopped—when you gave up coming to the office so you could be at home. Maybe that was a mistake.'

She shrugged. 'I don't know. I wanted it at the time, but then I suppose we both thought I'd get pregnant straight away—I mean you do, don't you? It happens. Why not to us? Only we didn't, and now I wonder if maybe it wasn't a good thing that it hasn't happened.'

'You don't want a baby any more?'

His voice was cautious, as if he felt he was treading on thin ice, but he needn't have bothered. It was a question she'd asked herself over and over again in the last few days, and she'd given up being sensitive about it. Instead she was just confused. She shook her head. 'I don't know. We've focused on it so hard I've lost sight of it. Does that seem silly?'

'Can't see the wood for the trees? No, it doesn't seem silly at all. It doesn't explain, though, why you didn't talk to me about the business once it was a success, or why you ran away. Particularly why you ran away without telling me, without talking it through with me. Didn't you think that, after five years, I had a right to know?'

The reproach in his voice cut her to the quick, even though she could see his point. 'It wasn't a question of rights,' she protested softly. 'I just—I'm not ready for this conversation, Rob. I don't know how I feel. I don't know what I think. I can't explain it to you because I don't know myself. If I did we'd all be a lot happier. All I can say is I'm sorry.'

She blinked away the tears that were threatening and picked up her tea again, wrapping her trembling fingers round the mug and holding it close, sheltering behind it.

He didn't say anything, just watched her, and she

could feel his eyes boring through her, looking for answers she wasn't able to give him. Wasn't able to give herself at the moment.

Midas lifted his head, his ears cocked, and she reached out a hand and fondled them. 'What is it, boy? Surely not another stray to rescue?'

'I can hear something,' Rob said. 'A tractor or something.'

He stood up, putting his mug down on the hearth and going to the window, peering out sideways towards the road. 'I can't see anything. Do any windows look that way?'

'In the kitchen. There's one that looks up the track. It's probably the guy at the top of the hill.'

They went into the kitchen and looked out over the featureless white landscape, but there was nothing to see except the odd tree stuck up out of the snow, white on one side, black on the other. It would have been beautiful if it hadn't been a trap, she thought, and wondered how they'd come to this, that being cut off with her beloved husband could feel like a trap.

She turned away. 'There's nothing there. I expect it's just a nearby farmer—the sound must travel on the wind. Come on, I'm cold. I'll see if the collie wants anything to eat.'

'Give her some warm milk and bread,' he suggested, and she looked at him as if he was mad.

'We've hardly got any for us.'

'We can manage without.'

'But you *hate* black tea and coffee—'

'I'll cope. She needs it,' he pointed out, and she remembered what it was about him that she'd fallen in love with, and regret filled her all over again.

She found a bowl, went back into the sitting room and silently crumbled a slice of bread into it, poured in some of their precious milk and added hot water to warm it.

'Come on, baby,' she crooned, pushing it under the dog's nose and tempting her with it. She lapped it weakly, then more eagerly, and when she'd finished she looked up at Laurie with gentle golden eyes and she was lost.

'Oh, lord, it's like Oliver Twist,' she said, choked. 'She's really hungry, Rob.'

'I know. Don't overdo it, though. A little at a time.'

Laurie stroked her head and felt the bones of her skull right under the skin. Poor, thin little dog. Thank God they'd found her.

Midas was standing beside her, his tail wafting gently, and she patted his great solid head and praised him for rescuing her. He licked her hand and jumped up on the chair beside his new friend, and she shifted to make room for him as he lay down.

Love at first sight, she thought, and remembered her and Rob. It had felt like that, at least for her, and when he'd taken her on to work alongside him she felt as if he'd turned a light on inside her and brought her to life.

She remembered the first time he'd made love to her—he'd laughingly conceded a point in an argument, but only if he could take her out to dinner. She couldn't remember where they'd gone or what they'd eaten, only that it had been wonderful, and afterwards he'd taken her back to his penthouse and stood with her in the dark looking out over the lights of London, and somehow with only the dim glow from outside to light them, the careful distance they'd maintained had melted away and they'd reached out for each other and found a happiness so exquisite she thought she'd die of it.

She'd realised then that she loved him, and she still loved him now, but things seemed to have got in the way and their happiness had faded to a distant memory.

'Touching, isn't it?'

His voice was deep and close behind her, and sent shivers down her spine.

'It didn't occur to me he was lonely,' she said, only too glad to change the subject that was filling her head and her heart to the exclusion of common sense.

'Maybe he didn't realise that he was,' Rob said softly. 'Maybe none of us realise what we're missing until we've had it—or lost it.'

Her heart pounded. Was he telling her he was lonely? That he missed her? Very likely—but would knowing that make a difference to him? Would it be enough to make him change his working habits? Probably not.

Midas lifted his head again and made a soft sound in his throat, half-way between a growl and a whine.

'I can hear the tractor again—it sounds closer,' Rob said, and she felt him move away from behind her. Her shoulders dropped with relief—or was it regret?—and she turned and followed him back to the kitchen. The tractor was nearly at the gate, pushing and heaping the snow out of the way, and as it came to rest at the gate the cab door opened and a man huddled up in thick outdoor clothes jumped down and came towards them slowly through the drifts, pushing a stick in ahead of him to feel the way.

'I'll let him in,' Rob said, but she fixed him with a look.

'No, I'll let him in, it's my house.'

He arched an expressive brow but she ignored it and went to the front door, opening it and leaning out to wave.

'Morning!'

'I saw the smoke—didn't know there was anybody here. Thought I'd come by and make sure you were all right.'

Come by? Just like that, with six-foot drifts across the track? Laurie stifled the urge to laugh. 'How kind of you, thank you. Mind the cars. They're there somewhere.'

'I'll be fine. You go along in, don't let the heat out.'

Heat? He must be kidding. Still, she closed the front door until she could hear him approaching, and then opened it again. 'Come in. I didn't expect any visitors today,' she said with a welcoming smile. She held out her hand.

He didn't smile. His face was craggy and lined, weathered with years of being out in just these conditions, and he tugged off a glove and stuck a calloused, icy fist into her hand. 'Iain McGregor,' he said bluntly, and looked over her shoulder.

'I'm Laurie Taylor,' she told him, and followed his gaze. 'This is Rob Ferguson. He's from London. He popped in yesterday and got stuck.'

'Aye.' He nodded at Rob, took his hand and looked around. Midas was barking on the other side of the door, and Laurie let him out.

'Shh. Good boy,' she said, and he sniffed and went back to guarding his girlfriend. She led Iain McGregor into the sitting room with Rob bringing up the rear, and offered him a cup of tea.

'I could manage a wee dram,' he said, deadpan, and Laurie's heart sank. The woman in the shop had suggested a bottle of whisky, but she'd declined and earned herself a disapproving look. Perhaps she should have succumbed. Maybe if she got out the wine—

Rob just smiled. 'I've got just the thing,' he said, and went out into the hall again. He shut the door, and a moment later she heard the front door close behind him. In the awkward silence that followed, she looked helplessly around and rubbed her hands together with false enthusiasm.

'Well, I must say it's a rare welcome to Scotland,' she said with a smile, and he grunted.

'The drifting's the worst thing. We need a warm day to melt the top, then it might get a wee crust. That'll help.' He looked past her and nodded his head at the dogs.

'I see the wee collie's found a bed.'

She looked at the skinny black and white dog snuggled up to Midas, and nodded. 'He found her under the snow this morning. She was nearly dead.'

'She's a stray. She used to come by ours and steal food, and m'wife used to put down the odd bit for her, but I got a new bitch a few months back and she hates her—chases her off. I wondered where she'd gone.'

'Does she have a name?' Laurie asked, and he looked at her in astonishment.

'Lord, no. I have enough trouble finding a name for ma ain dogs, no mind the strays! But she looks like she's found a home.'

Laurie nodded slowly. 'I think so. Midas seems to have adopted her.'

'You'll have pups.'

She shook her head. 'No. He's been done—he was a rescued dog. It's one of the rules.' She heard the front door go again, and looked up to see Rob, the arms of his dark blue coat white to the elbows with snow, coming into the room with a grin and a bottle of malt whisky.

'Duty free,' he said cheerfully. 'Laurie, where are the glasses?'

They drank half of it between them, the farmer putting away a good bit all by himself, and under its influence he mellowed a little and settled back into the settee and told them about the area and a little of its chequered and violent history, including some of the local place names and their meanings.

'So what does Little Gluich mean?' Laurie asked, still curious about the name, and he chuckled.

'Ah, well, now,' he said slowly. 'Either a small, sticky place, and when the snow thaws you'll understand that one, or a wailing of women. In the uprising there was a lot of raping and pillaging went on. M'wife reckons they were wailing because the cottage was too far out of the way and they got missed out. Mysel', I'd go for the small, sticky place. I've had the tractor stuck a time or two down by here.'

Laurie chuckled. 'I'll hold fire on my judgement until I know it better,' she said.

He nodded, and looked regretfully at his empty glass.

'More?' Rob offered, but he shook his head.

'I must away home. M'wife will be fretting—dinner'll be on the table. Are you all right for fuel?'

'Not really,' Laurie confessed. 'If the power stays off so we can't use the central heating, I've only got the coal in that bag.'

'What about the wood pile?'

'Wood pile?' she said blankly.

'Aye—by the end of the croft. Just round the back there.'

He pointed through the wall, and she shook her head. 'No wood pile. At least, I didn't see one. That's where the bag of coal was.'

'They might've run out afore they went. I'll bring you some logs. The power could be off for days.'

Oh, great, she thought, and had a sudden vision of herself down here in the chair with the dogs on top of her while Rob stretched out full length on the settee.

Or not. She gave the dogs a disgusted look. They could probably manage to lie by the fire for the night, she thought drily.

Iain McGregor went, trudging his way back through the path he'd forced through the snow earlier, swaying slightly under the influence of rather too many wee drams, and she evicted the dogs from the chair and made them go outside to relieve themselves.

Midas went more or less willingly, but the little collie looked scared to death, as if she was going to be kicked out into the snow and left to die again.

'Oh, sweetheart,' Laurie said softly. 'Don't be afraid. Come on back in and have something to eat.'

She fed her again while Midas sniffed around the spot where he'd found her, and she swallowed down another bowl of bread and milk with some of his dry food mixed into it.

'What are you going to call her?' Rob asked, coming back in with Midas from seeing McGregor off.

'I don't know. Something soft—quiet. Bella? Saffron?'

'Saffron's yellow. She's black and white.'

'Minstrel?'

'Minstrel. What do you think of that, little one?' Rob crouched down and stroked her, and her tail waved gently, but she was shaking. They were too close—too much too soon for the little stray.

'Let's go back by the fire,' she suggested, and took a pan of water back with them to make fresh tea. 'I don't know about you,' she said to Rob, 'but I could do with sobering up. That stuff's lethal.'

He gave a slight chuckle. 'Your face when he suggested a wee dram—it was priceless.'

Laurie smiled wryly and told him about the woman in the shop. 'I should have succumbed. It would have been much less expensive than the malt.'

'It was duty free, so I doubt it. Anyway, it hardly matters. He's going to bring us logs. It's a small price to pay.'

'He might charge me.'

Rob grinned. 'He might well, but it's better than freezing to death or burning the kitchen table.'

They both laughed, and then suddenly the atmosphere changed, became charged with tension, and her breath caught in her throat and she looked hastily away. The pot of water was boiling, and she made tea with trembling fingers and tried not to think about the look in his eyes or the need that was rising in her with every moment in his company.

She wouldn't give in to it—she couldn't. Not now. She had to think this through, and falling for his charm wouldn't help her one tiny bit.

Damn. He was getting closer, he knew it, but just when he thought the barriers were coming down, up they went again and he was back to square one.

He sat obediently in his corner of the settee, drank the tea she handed him—with a dribble of the rationed milk—and said nothing. He wasn't going to make it easy for her. Why should he? She'd left him, let her deal with the awkward silences and the raging attraction that still burned between them.

She curled up at the other end of the settee and put her nose in her tea, and he watched her out of the corner of his eye and ached for her. She was slender, but she curved in all the right places, and there was something about the fine angle of her jaw and the stubborn set of her soft, full mouth that made the ache much worse.

They'd had so much, he thought with regret. Too much to throw away so easily. He wouldn't give in. He couldn't. She was coming home with him if it killed him—assuming he didn't die in the meantime of cold or starvation—or frustration, he thought wryly, watching her still.

She shifted slightly, and her fine wool jumper pulled across the side of her breast and he had to stifle the groan of need.

'I'm going to look for these logs,' he said, getting up and putting his mug down on the hearth almost untouched. 'I brought my boots in. Do you want me to try and dig out the garage so you can get to it when the power's back on?'

'That would be good,' she said, a little too fast, and he almost regretted suggesting he went out. Staying in there with her was clearly unsettling her, and that was good—except it was unsettling him, too, and he needed to go and cool off if he was going to win this one.

He pulled on an extra jumper, donned his coat and boots and went out into the biting wind. Cool off? He'd freeze to death, he thought, putting on his gloves from the front of the car and wielding the grillpan like a machete to slice his way through the snow.

It probably wasn't very efficient, but it warmed him up and took the edge off his frustration. He made his way to the garage door, scraped away the snow and found the shovel, then started to tackle the path back to the house. By the time he reached the door he was hot and tired, and frustration was the last thing on his mind.

Iain McGregor brought the wood at two, and tipped it by the gate. They spent the rest of the afternoon, what little there was of it, moving the logs by hand one at a time into the lee of the cottage.

The wind was shifting, swinging round to the north, and there was a bitter edge to it now that cut right through them even though they were working. It carried the snow like tiny needles of ice that sliced at any bare skin it contacted, and Laurie huddled inside her inadequate coat and wondered if she wouldn't be better off inside with a saw explaining the table to the owners.

Still, eventually it was all shifted over to the side of the cottage out of the drifting snow, and they went back inside, stamping the snow off their boots. Rob turned her and brushed the snow off her back with firm, long strokes, and the touch of his hand made her want to whimper. It was so brisk and businesslike, not at all what she wanted, and yet she could have stood there for hours just to have him touch her at all.

You sad case, she told herself, and returned the favour, sweeping the thick snow from his shoulders and back, resisting the urge to explore the solid, muscled contours of his spine.

'I need the loo,' she muttered, hanging her coat on the peg, and opened the bathroom door only to let out a shriek.

'What?'

'The cat flap,' she wailed. 'We forgot to block it.'

'And?' He peered over her shoulder. 'Ah.'

Ah, indeed, she thought. The wind, veering round and picking up, had blown it open and driven snow straight in in a heap on the bathroom floor.

'I'll get a dustpan and scoop it into the bath,' he said, and while he was doing that she pulled the snow out of the little tunnel in front of the cat flap, pushed it firmly shut and locked it. What a crazy place to put it, she thought, but maybe it wouldn't be if the wind wasn't from that angle—or if she'd thought to lock it in the first place. After all, no self-respecting cat would have used it in the snow, so it probably hadn't been a problem in the past. She stuffed a towel in the hole to act as insulation, and watched Rob.

Using the dustpan as a scoop, he scraped the snow up and dropped it in the bath, and then straightened.

'It might melt eventually. Fancy a cup of tea now your friendly farmer's brought us some milk?' he suggested, and she gave a strangled laugh.

'Sounds good. Make lots, I'll bathe in it to thaw out. Now hop it, I need the loo,' she said, and pushed him out of the door. The bathroom felt freezing, even huddled in her thick clothes, and she found herself wishing fervently that the heating could come back on. Apart from the fact that the loo seat wouldn't be quite so cold, it would mean she could go upstairs tonight to bed alone—and get away from him and his lopsided grin and his cobalt blue eyes and his sexy charm.

Getting away from him was fast becoming a priority, because otherwise she was going to fall victim to that lazy, cheeky grin and the potent sex-appeal that came off him in waves, and that would never do.

CHAPTER SIX

THE power didn't come back on, but then she might have known she wouldn't be that lucky. They struggled through the rest of the day—at least, Laurie struggled. Rob seemed only mildly irritated, but then he was able to burn off some of his energy by being physical.

The coal was getting low, and they were going to need it to keep the fire on overnight, so he stood a paraffin lantern in the window to light the path outside, found an axe round the corner where the coal had been and chopped up some of the logs and stacked them in the hall.

He'd abandoned his cashmere coat in favour of a chunky Aran sweater, and Laurie stood in the shadows of the sitting room and watched the swing of the axe and the powerful flex of his shoulders under the thick woollen sweater, and ached for what she'd lost.

'You'd lost it already,' she reminded herself, and tried not to think about their beautiful, elegant house in London and the warmth of the central heating and the comfort of their big bed with the luxurious downy quilt that snuggled round them like a lover.

Never mind Rob snuggled round her, his big body pressed against hers, or turning her to face him and making love to her until she begged for mercy.

Minstrel was up out of the chair, sniffing and circling the floor, and Laurie opened the door and let both dogs out for a quick run. Rob was just coming in with the last armful of chopped logs, and as she dragged in a much-needed lungful of air she could smell the sweet scent of the pine and the warmth of his body, and the combination made her body yearn for him.

'You've done enough, haven't you?' she said. 'Don't get cold.'

He snorted. 'Not a chance—but the wind's got a real edge to it, so I'm going to stop. I don't want frostbite and we've got enough logs for a day or so.'

The dogs sniffed around, did their business and were back in in seconds, sneaking onto the chair and snuggling down again before Laurie could suggest the hearth-rug.

'Supper?' Rob said hopefully, bringing in some of the wood from the hall and piling it on the fire. She thought through her purchases and wondered what they could cook successfully. They'd had beans on toast for lunch—hardly haute cuisine, but filling and tasty. It was about the limit of her stock of instant food, but at least they had milk now since Iain McGregor had been.

And there was a fruit cake from his wife, too. Perhaps they could have that for pudding. As for the main course—

'I don't suppose you've got anything easy, in a tin?' Rob said, peering over her shoulder into the sparsely furnished cupboard.

'Not really,' she said, wishing she was into convenience foods more and didn't tend to cook everything fresh. She hadn't really factored in the weather, and she certainly hadn't anticipated being snowed in with a big, hungry man! 'I've got more of that pasta thing we had last night, but I don't know how well you can cook it over heat instead of in the oven. I could try a risotto. I wonder if that would work.'

'I guess we'll find out,' he said, straightening. 'Come on, it's cold in here. Let's go and experiment.'

Actually it worked, more or less, and they had cold grated cheese over the top and put the plates in front of the fire for a moment to melt it.

'Not bad,' he said, manfully swallowing the rather uneven rice complete with crispy bits where it had stuck on the bottom of the pan. 'I've had worse.'

She couldn't imagine where, but she didn't argue. It was the best they could manage under the circumstances, and at least they wouldn't starve. The flavour wasn't bad, she supposed, and it certainly smelled good.

She glanced over her shoulder at Midas and Minstrel, who were watching them both hopefully. 'Forget it,' she advised them, and Midas grunted and dropped his head. After a moment Minstrel settled again, but she still watched hungrily, and Laurie weakened and gave her the last few bites mixed with some dog food. Midas had a tiny scrape, just so he didn't feel left out, but she was worried about Minstrel.

'She'll be fine,' Rob said, reading her mind again. 'Tea and cake?'

She was about to tell him to get it himself when she realised he was. The pan was on to boil the water, the cake was out and cut into wedges, and she felt churlish and petty. What was it about him that had her permanently on edge?

'They'll have to sleep on the floor tonight,' she said. 'I'm not going upstairs, and I'm not lying on the hearth-rug, either.'

'So sleep with me on the settee,' he said reasonably, and her heart thumped.

'No way,' she retorted, wishing that she could allow herself the luxury.

He sighed and rammed a hand through his hair. 'Laurie, we'll be fully dressed. We've been married for five years. I think I can manage not to assault you in the night.'

It wasn't him she was worried about, she thought with a strangled laugh.

'We'll see. I'll try and talk them into the hearthrug later.'

They weren't having any of it. Midas whined, and Minstrel looked at her with such huge reproachful eyes that she felt like a murderer.

'Oh, have the damn chair,' she grumbled. 'Rob, shove up. I'll sit at the end.'

'You don't have to sit—'

'Yes, I do.'

He sighed, but he curled his legs up to make room for her, and she sprawled across the corner of the settee, the quilt tucked up round her ears to cut out the draught from behind her. She was warm enough, but after a while her legs ached and her back ached and she just wanted to lie down.

'You're being silly,' he pointed out after half an hour of shuffling. 'Come here.'

His voice was soft and coaxing in the firelight, and she was so uncomfortable she gave in and lay down stiffly beside him with her back to him and a discreet gap between them that gravity did its best to dispose of.

'It's only so I don't have to turn the dogs off the chair,

so don't think I'm giving in,' she said, contrary to the last, and she heard a muffled chuckle against her shoulder.

'Of course not,' he said soothingly, and his arm came round her waist and tucked her up against him into his glorious warmth, doing away with the gap, and she sighed with relief and something else that she didn't want to think about too closely and let herself relax.

It felt wonderful to hold her. She was soft and warm, her earlier tension gone, and the hair that tickled his nose smelt of her shampoo, familiar and comforting.

Oddly, he didn't feel aroused holding her, just contented. Normal. He tried to remember the last time he'd slept with her in his arms, but he couldn't. He could hardly remember the last time he'd slept with her, never mind in his arms. Three weeks ago? Two and a half? Ages, anyway, and it had been more about trying to achieve conception than holding her or loving her.

He swallowed a lump in his throat, and his arm tightened involuntarily around her. Where had they gone so wrong? He didn't know. He just knew that holding her like this felt more right than anything had felt for a long time, and gradually his exhausted body relaxed and he fell into a deep, dreamless sleep.

He was aroused. She could feel it, even through their clothes, because her bottom was snuggled right into him and they were so close she would have been hard pushed to get a credit card between them.

He was still asleep, his arm over her waist a dead weight, and she could feel the soft puff of his breath against her hair as he exhaled. His chest rose and fell slowly against her back, and she lay there for a few minutes just enjoying the warmth and the comfort of his body.

Human contact, she told herself, that was all it was, but she knew in her heart it was more than that. She still loved him, of course, but there was nothing she could do about it. Unless he changed drastically she couldn't live with him again, no matter how much she might miss certain aspects of their relationship and their life together.

What a lonely thought.

She turned back the quilt and lifted his arm carefully, wriggling out from under it and tucking him back in before straightening up. The dogs were on their feet, tails waving gently, and she crept out into the hall with them and let them out into the still, silent dawn.

The sky was crystal clear, the sun just edging over the horizon as she watched, and she huddled her arms round her and looked out over the snow-covered landscape and sighed with contentment.

It was beautiful. The sun was just high enough now to touch the tops of the hills on the horizon, turning the snow to gold, and in the distance she could hear a dog bark. Midas and Minstrel lifted their heads, but they didn't bother to respond. Too busy trying to convince her to come back inside and feed them, she thought with a smile, and took them into the chilly kitchen and gave them breakfast.

Minstrel wolfed hers down, as if she was afraid she'd lose it, and Laurie stroked her and soothed her while Midas finished his at a more leisurely pace. 'You'll get indigestion if you eat that fast, silly girl,' she told the dog gently, and she looked at her with liquid gold eyes and Laurie smiled. Such trust. Poor little thing. It was humbling.

She filled a pan with water and went through to the sitting room, prodded the fire into life and set the pan on it to heat. It would take ages, and in the meantime all she had to do was watch Rob sleeping.

Or not.

His eyes were open, studying her, his face serious.

'Good morning,' she said lightly, ignoring the thump of her heart.

'Morning. How did you sleep?'

'Wonderfully. You make a good pillow. I'd forgotten.'

He snorted softly and rolled onto his back, crossing his legs at the ankle and folding his arms under his head. He looked big and broad and vital, a healthy male in his prime, and after waking up close to him she really didn't need to see him looking quite so good. She could still feel the imprint of his body against her back.

She busied herself with the tea that wasn't quite ready, and tried to ignore the sounds of him stretching and yawning and unfolding his long frame from the makeshift bed.

'I'm going to wash. I don't suppose the power's back on, is it?'

She shot him a look. 'Would I be making tea on the fire if it was?' she asked patiently, and he gave her a cockeyed grin.

'Never can tell. You do some funny things.'

She glared at him, and he smiled and walked out, closing the door behind him with a soft click. She growled under her breath, and Minstrel lifted her head and whined.

'Oh, sweetheart, I'm sorry,' she crooned. 'Just ignore me. The place is freezing and the water's still ice-cold, and I want a hot bath and my own bed at night—and that man out of here before he drives me mad.'

'That man' came back in then, a towel slung round his neck, and rummaged in his suitcase for clothes.

'I'm going to have a shower,' he told her, and she stared at him as if he was quite insane.

'Are you all right?' she asked, a little stunned.

He laughed. 'I don't know. I'll tell you later. A nice hot cup of tea would be good in a minute.'

He wasn't long. She heard a yelp and a gasp through the thickness of the doors, and stifled her smile. She made him a big mug of tea, with a generous slosh of their newly replenished milk, and put it on the hearth to keep warm while she waited for him to return.

He came through the door briskly and still naked, scrubbing his wet body with the towel, and with utter disregard for her presence he came over to the fire, finished drying and then put his clothes on while she tried desperately not to give in to temptation and look at him.

Not that she hadn't seen it all before, but it did nothing for her composure to have that beautiful body standing right beside her as he tugged on his clothes!

'Your tea's there,' she told him, scrambling to her feet and getting out of the way. 'I'll just go and wash.'

'I wouldn't bother to shower,' he said crisply. 'I think the water is actually frozen in the pipes—I swear there were ice crystals in it. I thought I was going to cut myself on it.'

She chuckled and went into the bathroom bearing the pan with its leftover inch of hot water. The room smelt of his soap and shampoo, familiar and rather enticing.

She shrugged, ran a bowl of cold water and put the hot into it, then stripped and washed quickly, trying not to fantasise about the jacuzzi at home. The power would be on soon.

It had to be—didn't it?

It came on at eleven, and they checked that the heating was working and then she looked towards the garage with its office above and sighed. 'I ought to check my email.'

'Can I check mine?' he asked. 'I probably have a thousand messages from Mike—he gets deranged if I'm out of contact for more than a couple of hours.'

She shrugged. 'Sure. Feel free. We can put the fan heater on flat out. It might take the edge off it until the storage heater's had time to charge up.'

It was freezing, of course, but while he checked his mail and answered a few of Mike's more pressing queries, she huddled over the fan heater and looked out of the window. It was a glorious day—too nice to be shut in an office. Suddenly her business held no appeal at all.

'There—all done. It's all yours.'

She glanced through her emails and shrugged. The sun was calling her, and nothing seemed as important as that. 'I'll do it later,' she said, closing down the machine. 'It's Sunday—day off. I'd quite like to go for a walk with the dogs up the track and see what the lane looks like.'

He nodded slowly. 'May I come too?'

'Of course you can,' she replied, surprised that he'd even asked. She'd expected him to come—hadn't for a moment thought that he wouldn't. So much for her new-found independence—he seemed to be taking it more seriously than she was!

They went back to the cottage, put on extra jumpers and socks, and set off with the dogs up the track over the thick, crushed snow left by the tractor treads.

Midas and Minstrel bounced around and barked and chased each other, and she and Rob strolled side by side, carefully maintaining a little space between them. It was probably coincidence as much as anything, because they were walking in the parallel tracks left by Iain McGregor, but nevertheless there was a formality about it that seemed to underline the gulf between them.

The lane, when they reached it, was completely blocked beyond Iain McGregor's farm entrance just a few yards up the hill, and downhill beyond their track.

'Look at the way the wind has sculpted the snow,' he said, but all she could see was that it was thick, too thick for there to be any hope of him driving out of there for days—maybe a week, even, or more, if the snow ploughs didn't come.

And that being the case, she knew she was going to die of frustration—if they didn't starve to death. Judging by the state of the cupboard, there was a real danger that might happen.

Ah, well. No doubt the dog food was perfectly wholesome, if not very appealing, and anyway, the frustration was bound to get her first unless he stopped looking so darned appealing. He hadn't shaved that morning—said the water was too cold and he'd cut himself.

She'd teased him and said it was a weak excuse, but he looked rugged and macho and even more delicious with dark stubble on his jaw, and the tiny crease in his cheek looked sexier than ever when he smiled. And of course, just as if he knew that, he kept on smiling.

They headed back towards the cottage, the dogs running ahead of them sniffing at the occasional patch of grass or heather that showed through where the snow had been scraped away by McGregor, and as they reached the gate Laurie hesitated.

'I really don't want to go back inside yet,' she said slowly. 'It's so beautiful out here, and without the wind it's not even very cold.'

'We could build a snowman,' he suggested with a lazy grin, and her heart flip-flopped.

'We could.'

'Start with a snowball and roll it,' he told her. 'I'll make the body, you make the head.'

It was hard to find any snow shallow enough to roll the ball through, but they managed, and within half an hour their snowman was built. They'd found a little bit of branch for his mouth, and two pebbles for his eyes because she wouldn't let Rob use their precious coal, and a chip off a log for the nose, but Rob refused to give up his silk scarf to tie round the snowman's neck.

Laurie scooped up a handful of snow and held it threateningly out. 'Take it off,' she ordered, struggling to hide her grin, but he just bent down and scooped up a bigger handful of snow and hefted it gently in his palm, rotating it, patting it into shape, his mouth kicked up into that sexy grin that did for her resolve.

'Make me,' he taunted her, and she lobbed her snowball at him.

He ducked and she missed, but his hit her with deadly accuracy, taking her breath away.

'Oh! That was freezing!' she shrieked, shaking the snow off her neck and laughing. 'That's it! War!'

She scrambled behind the garage, taking a handful of snow with her and lobbing it at him as she went, but her aim was wild and missed him by miles. She shot round the corner, spent a few moments making a little pile of missiles and then cautiously poked her head round the side.

'Gotcha!' he yelled, laughing, and she ducked back and wiped the snow off her face. The sneaky rat had moved, taking up a position behind a hummock that had to be a bush, but she knew where he was now and she wouldn't be caught again.

She crept out of her hiding place, missile in hand, but there was no sign of him. 'Well, where the—aagh!'

He laughed as she spun round and brushed the snow off the back of her head. 'That's cheating!' she said, trying not to laugh, and grabbing a handful of snow she ran at him full tilt and knocked him over, shoving the snow down his neck while he laughed and yelled and tried to push her away.

Not hard. Not hard at all, in fact, and after a moment he lay motionless, his fingers coming up to wipe the snow gently away from her cheek.

'Laurie?' he murmured, and she scrambled to her feet, her heart pounding.

'Look at us, we're covered in snow! We'll have to shake it off—'

'Laurie.'

She stopped and turned towards him, speared by the blue lasers of his eyes. The heat in them made her trem-ble, and she turned away, calling the dogs and heading back to the cottage. Dear God, she wanted him. Wanted him to touch her, to hold her, to make love to her.

Idiot. What did she think she'd been doing? Playing with fire, not ice. Fire, hot and dangerous, tempting her, tormenting her, drawing her relentlessly in, but nothing had changed. Their relationship was still on the rocks, and this wouldn't solve anything.

He was right behind her, catching the door as she shut it and following her inside. She went into the bathroom and shut the door firmly, hoping he'd take the hint. He did. At least, he didn't follow her. She took her coat off with trembling hands, shaking it out over the bath and then hanging it on the hook near the radiator.

'I'm going to have a bath,' she told him through the closed door. 'Just in case the power goes off again.'

He grunted something, but she couldn't hear it. He was in the kitchen. She could hear him moving around, talking to the dogs, filling the kettle. She ran the bath and climbed in, eyeing the lock on the door nervously. It wasn't very substantial, the slightest pressure would open it. Was he likely to come in?

Please, no, she thought desperately, but he did, his earlier reticence clearly overcome. He walked calmly in, set a mug of tea and a piece of cake down on the little rack over the bath and went out again without a word, leaving her more confused than ever.

She wondered if he'd come in again, but when he didn't she relaxed and sipped her tea and lingered in the bath, enjoying the hot water and coincidentally hiding from her next encounter with him. She didn't know what it would hold, or how she would deal with it, but she was sure it could only bring her heartache.

Regardless, she couldn't hide in there all day, and the room still wasn't exactly warm. She climbed reluctantly out of the bath, towelled herself briskly dry and realised she hadn't brought any clean clothes in.

Idiot. She stuck her head round the door and saw the sitting room door was closed. He must be in there with the dogs, she realised in relief, and ran upstairs into her bedroom. She dressed quickly in a fine wool sweater and her favourite dark trousers. She looked good—too good for a quiet afternoon by the fireside with two grubby dogs. She knew that—she just wasn't sure why she'd done it, and she didn't really want to examine her motives.

She'd just picked up the hairdryer when there was a tap on the door. She scraped her wet hair back from her face and opened the door, and he looked down at her with searching eyes.

She swallowed hastily and stepped back. 'What is it? I have to dry my hair.'

'I'll do it for you.'

He took the brush from her hand and pushed her gently into the chair, then started to ease the tangles out. It was a slow process, but he worked patiently without tugging it, and all the time her nerves were drawn tighter than a bowstring.

He did nothing, though, to alarm her. Said nothing, did nothing, just brushed her hair again and again in the stream of warm air until it hung smooth and glossy around her shoulders. He threaded his fingers through it, sifting it, letting it fall like a silken curtain, over and over again. She felt the whisper of his fingers against her skin, infinitely gentle, teasing, tormenting her, and then suddenly, abruptly, he dropped his hands and stepped back.

Now what? she wondered, but apparently again it was nothing. Nothing yet, at least.

He put the brush down beside her, unplugged the hairdryer and coiled it up and went to the door, his face unreadable. 'I'm making fresh tea if you want some.'

'Thanks. I'll be down in a minute,' she told him, and for some reason she found herself putting on a touch of make-up with fingers that trembled slightly. Just tinted moisturiser, because her skin was dry after being out in the sun, and a little lipstick because her lips were chapped—ditto, and then a touch of mascara because without it her eyes looked unbalanced because of the other two.

Nothing to do with the man downstairs who had seen her in every conceivable state of dress and undress in the past five years.

Of course not.

She went down to the kitchen and found him there with the dogs at his feet, looking hopeful. He was cutting up vegetables, slicing onions and carrots and parsnips, and there were potatoes boiling on the hob.

'I'm getting supper,' he told her, and she blinked in astonishment.

Rob, cook? She had no idea that he could. She retreated to the other side of the table with her mug of tea and sat watching him.

'So what are we having?' she asked, wondering why he was making supper at something after three in the afternoon.

'Roasted vegetable flan in a mashed potato case with white sauce, and that naughty tin of syrup sponge with instant custard that I found lurking in the cupboard.'

'Sounds lovely,' she said, suddenly hungry.

'Washed down with that bottle of wine you had stashed at the back behind it,' he added, and she felt herself colour a little guiltily.

'Ah.'

'Ah, indeed. Saving it for a rainy day?' His face was

deadpan but there was a teasing smile in his eyes that made her go weak at the knees.

'Sort of.' Actually she'd got it to celebrate her great escape, but at the end of the day she hadn't really felt like celebrating, oddly. More drowning her sorrows, and she'd felt that wasn't a very sensible thing to do. It might be the thin end of the wedge, and anyway, she'd never been much of a one for drinking alone.

'Want a hand with anything?'

'Nope. I can manage. You just sit there and drink tea and talk to me.'

'What about?'

He shrugged. 'You could tell me about your business.'

So she did, explaining how she'd got into it, how it had expanded, how she'd got her name known.

'I built a website, and people seemed to like it. They contacted me for help and information, and that was it. I offer a service, people buy it, I give them what they want.'

'Simple, really.'

She laughed. 'Not always. People can be very hard to please.'

He snorted. 'Tell me about it. You ought to let me see what you've done. You might be able to do something for one of our companies.'

'I have.'

He froze, knife in hand, and stared at her. 'You have?'

She nodded. 'The New York office's new offshoot. Mike contacted my website. Ironic, really. He was very pleased with it.'

'I know,' Rob said slowly. 'He showed it to me. It's good. He didn't say it was you.'

She grinned cheekily. 'He didn't know. I didn't think there was any point in telling him.'

'All part of the independence thing?'

'More not wanting to look like nepotism. I wanted it to be me, for myself, not because I was your wife.' She shrugged. 'It was fine. He was happy, I was happy. It wasn't like I was cheating you.'

'No.' He dropped the last carrot into the roasting pan and put it in the oven, then poured himself another mug of tea and sat down opposite her. 'You look lovely, by the way,' he said softly, and she felt warm colour brush her cheeks.

'Thank you,' she murmured, and her voice sounded a little breathless. Rats. It was all part of the charm offensive, of course, but suddenly she found she didn't care. What did she have to lose? It didn't matter if she succumbed. They were married, after all—except that now, because she'd moved out, somehow there was an edge to it that made it more exciting. And even if she succumbed, it changed nothing. He still worked ridiculous hours, and he always would.

She watched as he prepared their meal, creaming the potatoes with egg yolk and butter, spreading the mash onto a baking tray, adding the white sauce to the vegetables and folding beaten egg whites into the mixture before piling it in the potato case, baking it until it was golden brown and fluffy like a soufflé.

While they waited between operations, they played chess with a set he'd found in one of the drawers of the dresser, and she beat him.

Only once, but it was a miracle and made her wonder if he was more on edge than she'd realised. How interesting. She hid the smile and let him challenge her to another game. He won it easily, because by then, of course, she was busy contemplating what he might have up his sleeve, and she wasn't concentrating.

Finally, though, the chess set was cleared away, the dogs had been fed and the meal was on the table.

It was delicious. The bottle of indifferent wine didn't do it justice, but she drank it anyway. It had a wonderfully mellowing effect—just enough to help her relax and enjoy his company.

They shifted to the sitting room after their wickedly sticky syrup sponge, and sat on the floor in front of the fire and finished the wine. The edge of the settee was hard, and so he moved her, pulling her into his arms so she was leaning back against his chest, her head on his shoulder, basking in the warmth of the fire and the mellowing effect of the wine.

She could have gone to sleep quite easily, except that she would have missed it and that seemed a shame, so instead she sat and revelled in the feel of his chest behind her and the slight rasp of his stubbled chin against her temple.

She couldn't imagine anything more blissful.

And then he bent his head and laid a gentle kiss on the corner of her mouth, and she turned her head and looked up into those amazingly expressive eyes, and was lost.

CHAPTER SEVEN

HE LOWERED his head slowly, his eyes half-closed, shielded from her, and his lips touched hers with the softness of a whisper.

'Laurie...'

He kissed her again, so lightly that if she closed her eyes she might have thought she'd imagined it. She felt the trace of his fingers over her cheek, her throat, under her ear in that sensitive spot that only he knew about. His lips moved, following the path of his fingers, leaving a heated trail that cooled in the air, fire and ice, unravelling her.

Then he lifted his head and leant back against the settee, his eyes closed, and she could feel his heart against her shoulder, matching the rhythm of her own.

She sat there for a minute, aching for him, needing the closeness they'd had and lost. Could they get it back? Was their marriage worth fighting for? She didn't know, but she wanted the answer, and there was only one way to get it.

She stood up, looking down at him on the hearthrug, one knee drawn up, the other leg stretched out towards the fire, his head tipped back watching her. Her heart was pounding slowly as she held out her hand to him.

'Come to bed,' she said softly, and his eyes flickered shut for a moment. When they opened, they blazed with a blue fire that stole her breath away.

He took her hand and stood up, then pressed it to his

lips. 'You go on up. I'll be with you in a minute. I'll sort the dogs out and put the fire guard up. I won't be long.'

He released her hand and she went, her heart thundering, making a detour into the bathroom on the way. She cleaned her teeth until they sparkled, and took off her make-up. There was nothing worse than mascara down your cheeks in the morning, she thought, giving her skin a last cursory swipe with fingers that trembled with anticipation.

Then she went upstairs, suddenly inexplicably nervous. She'd been to bed with her husband countless times before. Why was tonight so different?

Because it was, she thought. For some reason it just was.

She closed the door behind her and leant on it. Should she undress? Be in bed? Sitting on the side? On the chair in front of the dressing table, brushing her hair? That was too hackneyed, and anyway, she didn't have the silk and lace negligée to do the scene justice. It would hardly work with a cotton nightshirt!

She wrapped her arms round her waist and shivered. It was still cold in here after the past couple of days, and she wasn't in a hurry to sit about half naked just to dress the set, so to speak.

Oh, rats. She felt as nervous as a virgin bride, if such a thing still existed. She had her doubts. She looked around. He'd brought the quilt up from downstairs at some point and put it back on the bed. It looked very tidy and intimidating.

Should she have the lights on or off? And her clothes—on or off? And what about perfume?

Oh, Rob, help me. How do you want me? *Do* you want me, or is it just habit and proximity?

The door opened softly behind her, pushing her in the back, and she moved out of the way and let him in.

He eyed her warily, and she realised with sudden insight that he was just as nervous as she was, for some crazy and inexplicable reason. Oddly enough, that gave her courage. She smiled up at him and pushed the door closed.

'I waited for you,' she told him softly. 'It was too cold to undress.'

His mouth quirked up at the side and he nodded slightly, then stood there for a moment. He seemed to be waiting for her to make the next move, but she felt suddenly shy. How silly, to be shy with her husband!

'There's a full moon,' he said quietly, and turned off the light. 'Look out there. It's beautiful.' The room was filled with an eerie silver gleam, cold and brilliant as it reflected off the snow, and after a moment she could see almost as clearly as before. She looked out over the ghostly white landscape and shivered. It was icy and mysterious, slightly sinister in a way, and she was glad she wasn't alone.

She turned back to him, searching his face in the moonlight that streamed through the open curtains.

He was still standing there, his stubble dark against his skin, and she reached out a hand and rasped it gently against the rough hairs.

'I'm sorry, I should have shaved,' he said, but she shook her head.

'No. I like it.'

'It'll hurt you.'

'It's only stubble, not razor wire. I'm sure I'll live.'

She moved closer, rising up on tiptoe and pressing a gentle kiss to his lips. 'Everything done downstairs?' she asked, and he nodded.

'Everything's done. I'm all yours.'

She smiled, her heart thundering. 'Good.' Then going up on tiptoe again, she cupped his hands around his face and lifted her lips to his once more. 'Make love to me, Rob,' she murmured, and with a ragged groan he tunnelled his fingers through her hair, anchored her head and kissed her back.

There was nothing tentative about him this time. She'd unleashed a tiger, and she was ready for him now. His mouth plundered hers, demanding her response, and she gave it to him a hundred-fold.

His hands left her hair, sliding down her shoulders, over her arms, coming to rest on the soft fullness of her breasts. A ragged groan rose in his throat, and he tucked his thumbs under the hem of her sweater and slid his hands up against her skin, dispensing with the catch of her bra and taking her breath away. His thumbs chafed her nipples, teasing them, making them ache for more.

She made a helpless noise in her throat and he lifted his head, stepping back and peeling off his clothes in a few short, impatient movements. Her sweater followed, the bra tangling with it and going too, then her trousers fell to her ankles and he pushed her down onto the edge of the bed, kneeling in front of her and removing them and the thick, snuggly socks she'd put on to keep her feet warm for the evening.

All she was wearing was a thong, a deep wine-red lace thong that left little to the imagination and brought another groan from deep in his chest. He slid his hand up from her foot, leaving a trail of heat up her leg until he brushed the back of his fingers against the tiny lace panel that hid her from his heated gaze.

She gasped, and he smiled grimly. 'Oh, yes,' he vowed, and she felt heat pool under his hand. He pulled her to her feet, easing her against him so she felt the slight chafe of his body hair against the softness of her skin. It was unbelievably exciting.

'Rob—'

'It's all right, Laurie,' he soothed. 'It's all right. Slow down. There's no hurry.'

He lifted her easily, kicking the tidy quilt aside and lowering her to the chilly sheet. Then he was beside her, his body heat warming her as his lips found hers again. Her fingers cupped his jaw, rubbing gently against the sensuous scrape of the stubble, rough against her palm and unbearably erotic.

His lips left her mouth, trailing fire over her palm, the contrast shocking a tiny gasp from her. He grunted with satisfaction and moved on, up her arm, over her shoulder, down, to take an aching nipple into his mouth and suckle deeply on it.

She bucked and arched against him, and he lifted his head and stared deep into her eyes. 'I love you,' he whispered raggedly, and she wanted to cry.

'Rob—please,' she breathed, and he stripped away the tiny scrap of lace; his eyes locked with hers in the silver moonlight as he moved over her.

'I love you,' he said again, and then they were one, moving together in a dance as old as time, and she felt whole again.

She'd forgotten what it was like to make love with her husband, she thought sadly. He was sleeping now, his head pillowed on her chest, his lashes dark against the silver of his skin in the moonlight. She rested her hand on his head, her palm curled round, her fingers threaded through the silky-soft dark hair that teased her skin, and thought about the past year.

All the times they'd tried to make a baby, that was all they'd been able to think about. This time, not thinking about a baby, or failure, or if it was just the right time, not too early, not too late, they'd been able to concentrate on each other.

It had been wonderful, but Laurie knew it was all part of the magic of the weekend that fate had handed them. When he'd turned up, she thought it was going to be a disaster and, true, her plans had gone well awry, but there was no way she could call what had happened between them a disaster.

It was going to make it all the harder, though, when he left.

She stroked his shoulder, sleek and firm, and he sighed and shifted, rolling onto his back and drawing her into his arms. He tucked the quilt round her with a tender gesture that brought tears to her eyes, and with a contented sound he settled back into sleep.

Laurie didn't sleep, though. Some time before dawn, she heard the snow plough come through, and she knew he'd be going.

She woke him with a kiss, and he turned towards her, taking her into his arms and wrapping her close against him. 'Morning, gorgeous,' he murmured in her ear, and then his mouth found hers again and for a while she forgot about everything except the magic of his touch…

They walked up to the lane after breakfast and, sure enough, it was clear.

'I suppose I'd better be getting back,' he said once they'd returned to the cottage, and she could see the businessman resurrecting himself in him. 'I missed all sorts of calls on Friday. I really should have been in the office.'

'Borrow mine,' she offered, suddenly reluctant to let him go quite yet, but he shook his head.

'No. I'll get back now. I probably need to go into the office tonight and sign things. We just have to arrange to get all your stuff shipped back at some later date. What are we going to do about the dogs?'

'The dogs?' she said blankly.

'Well, they need an estate car, and I'm not happy about you driving in this weather. I suppose you could wait a few days and come when it's cleared—'

'Rob, I'm not coming back,' she said, and he looked at her in astonishment.

'What? What do you mean, you're not coming back? Of course you're coming back.'

She shook her head. 'No, I'm not. Nothing's changed between us. You still work too many hours, you're away too much, and I don't need that. I can't deal with it. I hate it—and when you're there, it's always pressured. I can't live like that any more, Rob.'

'But—' He broke off, stabbing a hand through his hair, and turned away, then turned back, his mouth a grim line. 'So what was last night all about, then?'

She gave a tiny shrug. 'I don't know. It just seemed right—'

'Because it *was* right. You're my wife—we're married, dammit. We belong together.'

'Not necessarily.'

'Yes, necessarily!' he ground out. 'For God's sake, Laurie, how could it have been like that last night if we didn't love each other? How could you have done the things you did with me if you didn't love me? That wasn't just sex, and you know it.'

She sighed and sat down at the kitchen table. 'I didn't say I don't love you.'

'So what are you saying?' he said, exasperated. He grabbed a chair and turned it round, straddling it, his arms folded on the back and his eyes pinning her like lasers. 'I don't understand, Laurie. What's going on in that head of yours? Tell me!'

'I don't know,' she said honestly. 'I just know I came up here to think, to find time to discover what I really do want from my life, and I don't know the answers yet. Until I do, I can't make any decisions.'

'But what about us?'

'Us is one of the things I need to think about, Rob,' she said gently. 'I don't know if there is an us any more—if there can be.'

'After last night?' he said incredulously. 'You still don't know, after last night? After the things I said?' His voice cracked, and he looked away, his jaw working. He'd shaved this morning, and she could see the muscle jumping under the smooth sheen of his skin.

'I'm sorry,' she murmured. 'It's not that I don't love you, because I do—'

'That's big of you. Don't overdo it,' he said sarcastically, but he was just lashing out in hurt, she knew that, so she let it go.

'Rob, I need time. I'm sorry if you can't accept it, but it's the way it is.'

'So I've just got to go away and leave you to get on with it?'

She nodded. 'Please.'

He was silent for a while, but then he lifted his head and speared her with his eyes. 'Can I see you?'

Again, she nodded. 'That would be lovely. I will miss you. I always miss you. Maybe this is the answer—we have our own lives and meet every now and again for the weekend.'

'Next weekend?'

'If you like.'

He sighed and shook his head as if to clear it, then stood up, spinning the chair and dropping it back under the edge of the table. 'Right, I'd better go and pack,' he said, and walked out.

She stared after him, hot tears stinging her eyes, and then folded her arms on the table and laid her head on them. She wouldn't cry. She wouldn't. Nor would she weaken. It would be so easy, but, as she'd told him, nothing had changed. He was a workaholic, and he always would be. Leopards didn't change their spots, and she wasn't sure she had the right to expect him to change what he'd always been.

She could hear him upstairs, moving around in the bedroom, gathering up his things, and she realised the sheets would smell of him that night and, even though he'd gone, she'd still be reminded of him as she lay alone in bed and ached for his touch.

He couldn't believe she was staying here. After last night, as well, after he'd opened his heart to her and told her he loved her—not once, but over and over again, so there was no chance she'd missed it.

He picked up his trousers and bundled them up angrily. Dammit, what was she trying to do to him? She couldn't just pick him up and drop him like some kind of toy!

And now he'd agreed to come back this coming weekend to torture himself further. He must be mad. Insane.

In love.

Oh, hell.

He gathered up the last of his things, ran downstairs and stuffed them into the suitcase. It would take him hours to dig out the car, of course. He'd only found one end of it, and he'd need to turn it round. Either that, or he'd have to reverse up the track.

Thank goodness he'd got traction control. He wasn't sure how well it would work under the circumstances, but it had to be better than nothing.

He pulled on his coat and boots, grabbed the shovel and went out and started digging. Maybe a little frenzied activity would settle his temper and calm him down before the drive. The way he felt right now, he was quite likely to write the car off before he even reached the lane!

He was angry with her. Laurie watched him out of the kitchen window, standing with her arms wrapped round her waist, holding in the ache. It took him ages, but finally the car was cleared of snow and he'd started the engine to warm it and clear the windows.

He was digging his way to the track now, snow flying in all directions, and then at last he linked up with McGregor's tracks and straightened up, stretching out his back muscles and flexing his arms.

His coat was long gone, put into the car for later, and he was looking hot and only marginally less angry.

She'd put the kettle on, and as he stomped his way back in, shedding snow in the doorway, she looked up and tried to smile.

'Coffee?' she offered, but he shook his head.

'No, I'll get on. I've got a long way to go.'

They stood there for a moment, her uncertain, him weighing the situation, and then finally she went up to him and stood on tiptoe and kissed him.

'Drive carefully. I'll miss you. Ring me when you get back.'

'OK. I might see you next weekend.'

Might? 'OK. Take care. I love you.'

His mouth tightened fractionally, and with a curt nod he turned away and strode over to the car.

She watched him go, reversing slowly up the track towards the lane, and the dogs whined and fretted and ran backwards and forwards between them.

'Come here, dogs,' she called, and closed the door once he was out of sight.

Only a few days to go and he'd be back.

She must be crazy.

'Right, you guys, cup of coffee and then I suppose I ought to dig the car out and go and buy some food. That sound good to you?'

Midas wagged his tail, but Minstrel was whining at the door and looking lost.

She could understand that. She stroked the dog's silky head and sighed. 'I know, sweetheart. I miss him, too.'

She brushed aside a tear, made herself a drink and settled down to write her shopping list.

* * *

It was a long way home. He only stopped once, somewhere in the Borders, and most of the way he was on the car phone, talking to his PA, and Mike, in New York—a very unimpressed Mike who'd been dragged out of bed to answer the first call—and anybody else he could think of so he didn't have to think about her.

And when he wasn't on the phone, he put one of his CDs on good and loud and nearly blew the speakers. Anything to drown out his thoughts.

Then finally he was home, if he could call it that. It seemed horribly empty and quiet, huge and unfriendly and soulless. No wonder she didn't like living in it on her own, he thought, and wondered if she might not have a point.

Whatever, she'd do what she wanted. She'd made that much clear. He carried his case up to the bedroom—*their* bedroom—and found the contents of his case from the New York trip dumped unceremoniously on the bed where he'd left it all on Thursday night. He put the case on the floor, chucked the other stuff after it and went back downstairs.

It was nearly ten o'clock, and he was bushed, but he ought to go into the office. New York was still open, just, and he really should be in touch with Mike.

He drove down into London to his office, parked under the block and went up, using his pass key to let himself in. To his surprise his secretary was there.

'Hi. I knew you'd come in, so I came back and got on with some work while I waited. Mike needs to talk to you about the coffee futures.'

'OK.' He sat in his chair, stabbed a few buttons on his phone and sat back.

'Coffee?'

'Thanks. I don't suppose there's anything to eat?'

'I can get something. What do you fancy? Chinese? Sushi?'

'A bacon sandwich,' he said with feeling. 'Mike, hi. I'm back in the office. Update me.'

Sue wandered off, muttering something about bacon sandwiches under her breath, and he tried to pay attention to his colleague. Obviously it had been a busy day on the world stock market, and there was a lot of catching up to do. He authorised some sales and some purchases, hung up and checked through his post.

There was mountains, of course, because he hadn't been in the office for nearly three weeks.

'Bacon sandwich,' Sue said, plonking it down in front of him.

He blinked at it. 'How the hell did you get that?'

'There's a greasy spoon round the corner. I went there.'

'You're a love,' he said fervently, and bit into it. He was starving.

'I got a cake and some chocolate as well while I was out.'

'I don't want chocolate.'

She grinned. 'No, but I do.'

He laughed softly. 'OK. More coffee?'

'In the jug. I'll get it.'

They worked for three hours, until even Rob thought it was unreasonable to keep her there so late, and he told her to go home and not come back until ten the next day.

He worked on for another three hours, then went up to the penthouse suite that he kept now for foreign visitors and crashed there for the rest of the night. He didn't fancy going home. It was too empty without Laurie, and he didn't feel strong enough to deal with it yet.

It was then that he realised he hadn't phoned her, but he couldn't really do it at four o'clock. He'd wake her—unless she was lying awake worrying about him.

He picked up the phone and then realised that her number was in his case at home and he didn't have it with him.

'Oh, hell. She'll manage,' he said, and stripped off his clothes, falling naked into the bed and sighing with exhaustion. He felt a prickle of guilt, but told himself it was her own fault she was up there in Scotland and not at home. If she'd been at home she would have known he was all right.

Except, of course, that he'd been going back to New York today. He sighed again, punched the pillow and was just going off when his mobile rang. He answered it, expecting it to be Mike, but it was Laurie.

'I'm back,' he told her. 'I've been in the office. I've only just stopped work—I'm in the penthouse. I'm sorry I didn't ring you. I forgot to get your number out of the case.'

'It doesn't matter. I didn't really expect you to phone, you never do. I just wanted to know that you were all right.'

'I'm fine. Tired, but I'm OK.'

'Good. Sleep well.'

'You, too.' He hesitated. 'I miss you,' he said, but she'd gone. It was probably just as well. There was such a thing as being too honest.

CHAPTER EIGHT

BUSINESS was brisk—so brisk that she didn't really have time to miss him, but still, she did.

She wondered if he was missing her. As she'd put the phone down on Monday night—well, Tuesday morning, really—she thought she'd heard him say so. He'd said something, but she hadn't quite caught it. It could have been 'miss you,' but it was unlikely. After all, if he'd missed her, he would have remembered to phone, wouldn't he, instead of immersing himself in work again the moment he was back?

No. He'd probably meant to miss her, but hadn't managed to fit it into his schedule, knowing Rob. Oh, well.

She settled into her new daily routine quickly. After all, it was much like her old one, just in a different place, and because of the cold and the snow there was no chance to walk the dogs in the morning as she'd walked Midas every day before she'd started work in London.

She made time to take them out during the warmer part of the day, though, and she played with them in the snow, although she was largely superfluous because they seemed to enjoy playing with each other better and she had the feeling they were only humouring her.

The snow was starting to thaw, but very slowly, and only where the sun hit it. The snowman they'd made was shrinking day by day, and as the weekend grew nearer she wondered if he'd still be there when Rob came back—if he came back. He'd sounded a little less certain as he'd been leaving, and now he was in New York. She knew that from his emails.

There was an element of reproach in them, she noticed with wry humour. He made sure she knew what he was doing every day, and she was sure he was visiting her website.

On Thursday morning she checked her email and found a message from him.

'Taken over a new company. It needs a website. Can we discuss it this weekend? See you Saturday morning. Rob.'

She messaged him back. 'No. Weekends are sacred. See you Saturday. Laurie.'

She'd see, she thought, just how serious he was about their relationship. If he brought the website up, she swore she'd kill him—but not until he'd made love to her at least a dozen times. She discovered she was looking forward to it with eager anticipation.

Not just the lovemaking, but the whole weekend. She stole some time away from her desk on Friday to go to Inverness and shop, and she bought all sorts of wonderful things for Saturday night.

She wasn't sure how long he'd be with her, or how tired he'd be. Was he flying straight in from New York to Glasgow, or driving up from London? She didn't know, he hadn't mentioned it. He might be flying from London. She looked on the Internet. There were several options, any of which he could take.

And he hadn't mentioned what time on Saturday morning, of course, so she didn't know when to expect him, but she doubted he'd leave New York before close of business. That would be too much to expect.

She changed the sheets that evening, just in case he

arrived early in the morning and caught her on the hop, and then had a bath and went to bed fizzling with anticipation tinged with a tiny bit of dread. What if it didn't work? What if last weekend had been a fluke? What if—so many what ifs.

She didn't sleep for ages, then the dogs woke her at five, barking furiously and scratching at the door.

Surely he couldn't have arrived so soon? She stumbled out of bed, shoving her hair back off her face so she could see out of the window, but there was no moon and it was impossible to see anything.

Her heart racing with anticipation, she went downstairs and let the frenzied dogs out of the kitchen—just in case it was someone else—then, tugging her dressing gown tighter round her, she opened the front door.

The dogs threw themselves out, wagging and barking furiously, leaping up and licking him, and she leant back against the wall and smiled.

'What a welcome,' she said when she could be heard over the kerfuffle, and he looked up at her and grinned, and her heart flipped over.

'You're early,' she said, and his grin tipped into a grimace.

'I caught the early flight to Boston, then the connection to Glasgow. I've been travelling for twelve hours. Take pity on me.'

'You love it.'

He snorted softly and reached for her, drawing her into his arms and hugging her hard, sighing against her hair. 'It's good to be here,' he said, and kicked the door shut behind him. His case was on the floor where he'd dropped it, and the dogs were sniffing round it and checking out his ankles and legs, just in case he'd been anywhere interesting.

'Do you want a drink?' she asked, but he shook his head.

'I could do with using the bathroom, then all I want to do is sleep. Go back to bed and wait for me.'

He dropped a kiss on her hair and released her, and she went upstairs and snuggled back under the covers. She heard water running, then him talking to the dogs for a moment, then the stairs creaked and he was there, slipping into bed beside her in the dark and taking her into his arms.

His skin was cool and slightly damp from the shower, but his mouth was hot and hungry, and his hands moved slowly over her, setting fire to her body inch by inch.

'I've missed you,' she confessed, and his arms tightened slightly round her.

'I've missed you, too. It's been a long, hard week.'

She slid her hands up and cradled his face. He hadn't shaved—deliberately? she wondered. Whatever the reason, she was pleased. She laid her mouth against his and nibbled gently at his lower lip, tugging at it with her teeth and bringing a low groan from deep in his throat.

'You're asking for trouble,' he murmured warningly.

'Mmm,' she said, and did it again. He bit her back, just gently, but hard enough to excite. Then his tongue stroked the tiny bruise, soothing it yet making it worse.

She couldn't help the little moan of need, and it just encouraged him. He moved on, his mouth hot and wicked, trailing over her body and leaving fire in its wake. Finally she could stand it no longer, and she gripped his shoulders, her nails digging into him, desperate for him to stop and yet to go on, to do more, to finish what he'd started so very, very cleverly.

'Rob—'

'Shh. It's OK. I'm here.'

He took her mouth again, trapping the cry of relief as he entered her, but the relief was short-lived, replaced by a burning need that threatened to consume her. She could feel the fine tremors in his body, feel the rigid control as he held back, waiting for her, leading her higher until she felt the first ripples starting.

He must have felt them too, because he groaned and stepped up a gear, releasing that devastating control and driving them both over the edge with a savage shout of triumph. Then he collapsed against her, his head on her shoulder, his chest heaving, sweat breaking out over his skin as he rested for a moment before shifting his weight slightly off her.

He didn't move far. She wouldn't let him. Instead he slumped to the side, his arms wrapped firmly round her, cradling her against his chest as he recovered. She could hear his heartbeat slowing, feel the lassitude creeping over him as he relaxed against her.

'I love you,' she said, and because she was so close to him she felt the tiny flicker of tension in him at her words.

'Good,' he said. That was all. Not 'I love you, too,' just 'Good.'

Stupidly, she felt hurt. She shouldn't have done. After all, she'd left him, not the other way round, and it was pushing it to expect him to be too open with his feelings. Last weekend, yes, because he'd thought she was going back with him. Now, though, it was a different story, and although she could understand, still she found it hurt.

She blinked away the stupid tears. She wouldn't do that to him—not cry and make him feel guilty. It wasn't fair. Oh, damn.

'I need the loo,' she said, wriggling out of his arms and heading for the door. She was in the bathroom before the first sob broke, but he must have heard her because he followed her in, turned her into his arms and held her while she cried.

'I'm sorry,' he said, sounding genuinely remorseful. 'I didn't mean to hurt you. Come back to bed.'

'I don't know why I bother with that lock,' she said with a sniff.

He glanced at the bathroom door in surprise. 'I didn't know you did. Want me to mend it?'

She shook her head and gave him a rather watery and lopsided grin. 'No. You wouldn't be able to bring me tea in the bath then.'

He chuckled and hugged her tighter against his side, then released her and followed her upstairs. Once back in bed he pulled her into his arms and kissed her gently.

'I do love you,' he murmured, and she snuggled closer.

'Good,' she said, hesitating a heartbeat before adding, 'because I love you, too.' She could feel his smile against her temple. He kissed her again, his lips warm against her face, and with a smile still on her lips, she fell asleep.

He slept until midday. She left him there and went down and fed the dogs, made coffee and sat in the kitchen and wished he'd wake up, but he was tired and she guessed he'd been having early breakfast meetings and late evening meetings and worked half the night, as well as working all day.

She wished he wouldn't push himself so hard. Apart from the fact that it left no time for them, he was going to kill himself, and she wasn't sure she was strong enough to sit back and watch him do it.

She made some preparations for their evening meal, starting the soup, peeling the vegetables and making the base for the pavlova and starting it off in the oven.

There was still no sign of him, so she took the dogs out into the garden and let them rip around a bit. It had thawed again in the night, the wind shifting round to the south-west, warmed by the gulf stream. All they needed was a little rain and the snow would be gone, she thought, and she'd see how right Iain McGregor was about the 'small sticky place,' although after last night maybe the 'wailing of women' was closer to the mark!

She heard her name and looked up, and he was leaning out of the window, looking rumpled and sexy and heart-stoppingly loveable.

'Morning, gorgeous,' he called, and she couldn't stop the little smile of pleasure at seeing him.

'Morning, gorgeous, yourself,' she replied, walking back to the house and standing on the drive beneath, looking up at him. 'Are you going to get up today?'

'I might—depends if I get a better offer,' he said softly, and she laughed.

'Not a chance. I've got coffee on.'

'I know, I can smell it. I'll be down in a moment. I've already washed.'

She went back inside with the dogs, and he ran down the stairs moments later, dressed in a fresh white silk shirt and trousers so beautifully cut they should have had a government health warning on them. A jumper was knotted round his shoulders, emphasising their breadth, and the whole package was enough to take her breath away.

She slid a mug of coffee across the table at him and cocked her head on one side. 'Breakfast?'

'Lunch? I can't remember when I last had a decent meal. I hate aeroplane food and lunch yesterday sort of got overlooked—I left the office at twelve, and breakfast was so early I don't even want to think about it.'

She chuckled. 'How about a BLT?'

'I thought you were vegetarian?'

'I am. You aren't, though, so I bought you bacon. I know you love bacon sandwiches.'

His eyes warmed and he gave her a lopsided little smile. 'A bacon sandwich would be wonderful,' he said softly. 'Thanks.'

He watched her while she cooked, humming under her breath and throwing things together with swift, economical movements. She looked good, he thought. Calm and composed, relaxed.

She hadn't been relaxed earlier, she'd been hurt and unhappy, and he felt a pang of guilt for upsetting her, but he'd just been wary about giving too much away. He might as well not have bothered, because she'd got it out of him anyway in the end.

He gave a silent laugh. She knew he loved her anyway, so what was the point of trying to deny or disguise it?

'Here you go.'

She slid a piled-up plate across the table at him and

sat down, one leg tucked up under her bottom the way she always did. She had a smaller plate, with what looked like salad in the sandwich, and she picked up one half and bit into it. She had beautiful, even teeth, he thought, almost translucent white, saved from perfection by a little chip on the corner of one of the top ones.

She'd come off her bike as a teenager, showing off, she'd told him, and he'd had an image of a sparkling, leggy girl with a row of admiring boys lined up to watch her with lecherous grins on their faces.

Absurdly he felt jealous because he hadn't been one of them. She must have been lovely. She was lovely now, certainly, and she'd been lovely at twenty-one.

She'd be lovely at sixty, he thought, but he wasn't sure he'd be around to see it. The thought was extraordinarily painful.

'Penny for them,' she said round a mouthful of sandwich, and he laughed and shook his head.

'No. You'll get an inflated ego.'

She smiled at that, blushing slightly, and he felt a rush of desire. It must have showed in his eyes, because the smile softened and her lips parted a little breathlessly. He wondered how soon he could decently hustle her back to bed, and decided decency had nothing to do with it. She was his wife. If he wanted to make love to her, it was nobody's business but their own.

'How about a little rest after lunch?' he suggested softly, and her smile widened.

'Sounds good.'

The rest of the sandwich nearly choked him.

It had been a wonderful weekend, she thought. He was flying from Edinburgh to Gatwick first thing on Monday morning, and would have to get up at three, so they had an early night.

No great hardship, she thought with a smile. They seemed to have spent a great deal of time in bed over the weekend. They'd walked the dogs on Sunday morning, though, taking them down to Dornoch and letting them run on the beach while they strolled hand in hand just above the surf line, and they'd had lunch in a pub on the way back while the dogs slept, exhausted, in the back of her car.

And amazingly, she thought, he hadn't once mentioned work except over lunch in the pub, to tell her how busy he'd been and where he was going next week.

London for the first couple of days, then Paris, then Hong Kong on Thursday and Friday and back in time to go to London again for Monday before heading back to New York on Tuesday.

'So you won't be here next weekend,' she said, perversely disappointed.

'No. I can't. Come to Hong Kong with me. You love Hong Kong.'

She shook her head in regret. 'I can't leave the dogs, and anyway, I don't have time. Too much to do.' It wasn't strictly true, but she didn't want him to think she could just drop everything and be at his beck and call. He had to believe in her new life, and he wouldn't if she was too ready to abandon it every time he crooked his little finger.

'Maybe another time,' he suggested, and she made some noncommittal reply and changed the subject.

They'd gone back to the cottage, made love again because they just couldn't seem to get enough of each other, and then after supper they'd gone back to bed so he could sleep before setting off for the airport.

Not that he slept much. She tried to remember when they'd last been so hungry for each other, but she couldn't. Still, she wasn't complaining. It was wonderful to spend so much time with him—quality time, real time, not coexisting as they'd done for the past eighteen months or so. It seemed a little perverse that now, when she'd left him and was seriously considering whether she could ever live with him again, they seemed to be getting on better than they had for years—possibly ever.

She woke at two thirty when his alarm went off, and they made love again before he tore himself reluctantly out of bed and left her. She got up at seven to let the dogs out, and went into the kitchen to make herself a cup of tea.

There, propped up against the kettle where he knew she'd find it, was a CD in a plastic case, a sticky note pasted onto the front of it. 'Have a look at this when you have time, and talk to me about it. We'll bounce ideas around. Thanks for a wonderful weekend. Love you. Rob.'

She looked at it curiously. What was it?

The new company, she realised. She'd forbidden him to discuss it, and he hadn't, but he'd left her the information anyway. She called the dogs back in, ran the bath and ate her toast while she wallowed, then went over to the office and put the CD into the computer.

It was interesting. Very interesting. She'd heard of the company, but their current website was atrocious and needed a good swift kick up the rear. It was just the sort of challenge she thrived on, and she found her mind chewing away at it while she got on with her other work.

He rang her at lunchtime to tell her he was back, and she told him her ideas.

'Sounds good. Can you put together something for me to look at?' he asked, and she agreed.

'Not yet, though. I've got some outstanding commitments I have to honour.'

'Sure. In your own time,' he said, then added, 'Any chance you could get to it later this week?'

She laughed. 'You don't give up, do you? I'll see. Now I have to go, work to do. Take care.'

'You, too.'

She did get to it that week—not because she had time, but because she made time by staying up late and working on it when a sensible person would have been curled up in front of the television with a glass of wine or a mug of hot chocolate. Anyway, she was happy to work to take her mind off missing him. She rang him at home on Saturday night to discuss the company, and he answered the phone sounding slightly groggy.

'Are you all right?' she asked.

He laughed a little tiredly. 'Sort of. I'm just back from Hong Kong—the flight was delayed. I was grabbing a quick kip. How are you?'

'Fine,' she said, feeling guilty. 'I'm sorry I woke you.'

'Don't worry. It doesn't matter, it's nice to talk to you. How are the dogs?'

'Fine. Missing you.' I'm missing you, she wanted to add, but she didn't. 'I've had a look at that website. It's truly dreadful, isn't it?'

He snorted. 'Tell me about it. The stupid thing is, the company's got so much to offer—so much life and energy and enthusiasm, so many good ideas. They're just not making it because frankly their marketing strategy stinks. So, did you come up with anything?'

She had, and she ran her ideas by him and wished she'd got a chance to show him, to discuss it face to face with the product there between them. She could zip the files and send him the information, but it wasn't the same as sitting side by side as they'd done in the old days and wrangling through a problem.

'It's a shame you can't come down,' he said. 'Meet them, see the set-up.'

'I can't,' she said regretfully, wondering if she could put the dogs in kennels for a short while. Midas would be all right, he was used to it, but she wasn't sure how Minstrel would take it. And anyway, she had too much to do. 'I'll email you and send you the web pages as an attachment. You can have a play and see what you think. Feel free to shred it.'

He chuckled. 'I'm not sure I'd dare.'

'You've never hesitated in the past,' she reminded him, and he laughed again.

'OK. Send them. I'll ring you or email you or something. Just give me five hours to sleep and I'll be up and running.'

She made a few more adjustments and sent the email, then did the curling up by the fire with hot chocolate thing. It didn't occupy her mind, though, and she realised just how much she was missing him.

She didn't want this, she realised, but on the other hand she didn't want to be imprisoned in his house, like a hamster in a cage, waiting vainly for him to take her out to play, and that's what it would be like. He was so busy they could hardly find time to talk on the phone, never mind be together. Even the weekends were busy.

If only she could get him to change his lifestyle, but she was more likely to succeed in teaching him to fly.

The phone rang again, and Rob struggled to the surface, swung his legs over the side of the bed and scrubbed a hand through his hair before reaching for the handset. Why hadn't he just unplugged the damn thing?

'Rob Ferguson,' he said shortly.

'Rob, hi! It's Andy. Is Laurie there?'

He sighed. Andrea Davies was one of Laurie's closest friends, and yet she obviously didn't know Laurie was away. What did he tell her? He shrugged. Only the truth. 'I'm sorry, Andy, she's not. She's in Scotland—having a little break. She's rented a cottage and taken the dog. Can I give you her number?'

'Oh—well, no, it doesn't matter. I was going to ask you both for dinner, but if she's away…' She trailed off, then added brightly, 'Not that that matters. Why don't you come on your own? It would be nice to see you. You haven't been round for ages.'

He groaned inwardly. Andy's parties were usually quite lively, and he didn't feel up to lively at the moment.

'It's only quiet,' she said. 'Tomorrow night. Do come, it'll do you good. Better than mouldering there on your own.'

She was right, he was mouldering. He hated being in the house on his own; it drove him crazy. It might do him good to go round to old friends.

'OK. Thanks. What time?'

'Eight?'

He thought of all he had to do on Monday, but he was in London at the start of the week and they only lived round the corner. Besides, he needn't stay too late. 'OK,' he agreed. 'Eight's fine. I'll look forward to it.'

Rather stretching the truth, but that was all part of the social niceties they all indulged in. He contemplated going back to sleep, but then thought better of it. He'd go and check his email, see if there was any word from Laurie.

There was—a quick note, disappointingly quick, and a collection of draught web pages and suggestions that were interesting and dynamic and thought-provoking.

It was nearly ten o'clock, but he rang her, as much to talk to her as anything, and they discussed her ideas at length. 'Are you at the machine?' he asked her, meaning to discuss the finer points of one of the pages, but she said no.

'I'm in the sitting room with the dogs. We were just watching the end of a programme and then I was going to bed. Do you want me to go over there and call you back?'

'No,' he said quickly. 'It doesn't matter, it'll keep. It's nice just to chat.'

'It is, isn't it?' she murmured, and he could picture her there, snuggled down in one corner of the settee, the dogs sprawled at the other end or the chair or on the hearthrug, snoring gently in front of the fire. Part of him ached to be there with her, but another, more sensible voice told him it was just a mirage, a moment out of time, like that ancient film of a Scottish village that disappeared and only came back for a day every year—or was it a hundred years?

He couldn't remember, but it was a fantasy world, not quite real.

Like his time with Laurie in Little Gluich. It wasn't

real. They were just playing, and if she came back, she'd be unhappy again, because he couldn't change his life. How could he? It wasn't possible.

They talked a little longer, and then he said goodnight and went back to bed. He was still exhausted, and he had a lot to do. There was a lot of catching up to do before he went into the office on Monday, and he'd agreed to go out to Andy's.

He'd forgotten to tell Laurie. Blast. He considered ringing her back, but thought better of it. She'd sounded tired. He'd leave her to sleep. He could ring her tomorrow when he got back and tell her all about it. There were bound to be people there that he knew.

'Rob! Darling, come in.'

Andy was wearing a lovely gown, long and slender and clinging in all the right places. Odd, how unmoved it left him.

He could hear music in the distance, playing softly, but no voices, and there were no other cars on the drive.

'Am I the first?' he said lightly, wishing he'd stayed at home and finished reading that report.

'The only,' she said with an apologetic smile. 'The others couldn't make it in the end—they've just rung to let me down. Never mind, it'll be nice and cosy. Come on through.'

She led him into the sitting room, and he looked round warily. The stage was set with candlelight and soft music, and through the door he could see the table laid for two. Just rung? Somehow he didn't think so. 'Where's Jonathan?' he asked, and she pulled a face.

'Away. He's always away, Rob. He's like you—never at home. I do most of my entertaining these days on my own. Still, that needn't stop us having a good time, need it? After all, Laurie's away too.'

He looked into her eyes and his heart sank. There was an open invitation there written in letters ten feet high, and he just wanted to run.

'I'm sorry, Andy, I don't play games,' he said firmly.

'Games?' she said, her voice light. 'What do you mean? It's just supper, Rob—old friends having supper together. What harm can there be in that?'

Nothing, of course, unless one of them moved the goalposts. Still, it took two, and he wasn't going to play ball, so she was on her own. Poor Andy.

Poor Jonathan.

Hell. Poor all of them. What was happening to them all?

'It's ready when you are. Shall we have a drink?' she asked with artificial cheer.

'I'm starving. I'd be quite happy to eat now, if I'm honest,' Rob said, only too pleased to hurry the evening along and get home. Lonely, hungry women were a dangerous breed, and this one was like a circling shark.

The food, predictably, was wonderful. Andy was a good cook and a superb hostess, and once she'd cottoned on that he really, genuinely wasn't interested, she switched tactics and started to unburden herself about Jonathan.

'He's just never here. It's awful, Rob. It wouldn't be so bad if we'd had kids, but we haven't, and it seems awfully lonely when he's away.'

'Maybe you need a job—like Laurie,' he suggested. 'She's a website designer. She's excellent.'

Andy looked stunned. 'Really? I thought she was just out of circulation—suffering from depression or something because of the baby.' She leant forwards and put a comforting hand on his arm. 'I'm sorry, Rob. I know how much you both want a baby, and I can truly understand that. Can't you do IVF or something?'

His personal fertility problems weren't something Rob considered dinner party fare, and he was suddenly glad it was only him and not a roomful of people, because Andy was well down the second bottle of wine with only minimal help from him because he was driving, and he had the feeling she would have expressed an opinion no matter who was in the audience. Nor did he want to hear any more about her marriage.

He removed his arm from under her hand and gave her a strained smile. 'I think that might be jumping the gun a little,' he said, and deftly changed the subject.

Still, it gave him pause for thought later. Andy and Jonathan were at the end of their rope, judging by the sound of it, and Andy was bored and lonely and playing dangerous games with her friends' husbands. He wondered if Jonathan knew, and decided he wasn't going to be the one to tell him.

Still, it was a lesson he would do well to pay attention to, he thought on the way home. He was lucky—his wife had simply found herself something productive to do, whereas Andy was just killing time with other women's husbands. Nevertheless, he'd lost Laurie, just as surely as Jonathan had lost Andy—or, at least, lost her fidelity.

At least Laurie had been faithful, but then he'd always thought they'd got something really special.

And now it might be gone, blown away in the wind due to neglect and his preoccupation with his business.

Was he really going to be able to let her go, if it came to it? He didn't see he had a choice. His schedule was hectic. That was the way it was, and if that meant he lost Laurie—well, then, he lost her. There was no way round it, and he'd just have to try and live with it.

He rubbed at the ache in his chest, but it didn't seem to want to go away. Indigestion, probably. Heartburn.

Or heartache?

He turned the music up and sang along, drowning out his suddenly very painful thoughts.

CHAPTER NINE

LAURIE was walking the dogs on Tuesday morning when she saw a woman feeding the sheep in the meadow above her cottage. She'd seen her before, but never to speak to. She went over to the gate and leant on it and smiled.

'Morning,' she said, and the woman looked assessingly at her and straightened up, acknowledging her with a nod.

'Morning. You must be Laurie. I'm Anne McGregor. Welcome to the area. I'm sorry you've had such dismal weather the past week.'

Laurie laughed. 'Oh, it doesn't matter. It was quite fun.'

'Iain tells me you had a visitor.'

Does he? Laurie thought, but didn't rise. 'Yes. We were very grateful for the logs, and the milk and the fruit cake.'

'No problem.' Minstrel had slipped through the gate and was sniffing Anne's ankles, and she bent down and patted her. 'Remember me, do you, lassie? She's looking well, the wee dog. Yours seems to have taken to her.'

'Oh, they're the best of friends. I hope I'm not upsetting anyone by taking her in?'

'Och, no! She's a stray! No one cares about the wee lass, and our dog hates her. No, I'm glad to see she's got a home. She's a nice wee thing.'

Anne leant on the gate and eyed Laurie up and down.

'You don't look like the country type,' she said frankly, 'so why here? Running away? That's why people usually come to Little Gluich.'

Laurie gave a slight smile. 'Just reassessing my priorities,' she said noncommittally. 'Having a little bit of a break.'

'Aye? Och, well, it must be nice to have the time. Are you busy later? You could drop by for a cup of tea, if you've a mind. I'm in all morning.'

Laurie thanked her. 'I might do that. I'll take the dogs home first, as yours doesn't like my little girl.'

She nodded, and Laurie left her there leaning on the gate, watching. She was torn about going round for tea, but she thought she ought to get to know her neighbours, if only out of gratitude. Iain had been very kind to her when she'd first moved in. Before they'd even met he'd cleared the track, and then brought them the logs, refusing to take any payment for them—even if it had cost Rob most of a bottle of malt.

She did one or two urgent jobs, sent a few emails and then put the dogs away before heading for the McGregors's farm. The back door was slightly ajar, and she tapped on it and went in, in answer to the hail.

Anne was up to her elbows in flour, and she jerked her head at the old range.

'Put the kettle on, we'll have a brew when I've finished this,' she said. 'Have a seat—just push the cat out of the way.'

She did, earning a dirty look for her pains from a dog-eared tabby with attitude. There was another one on the back of the stove, on a pile of washing that was airing, and yet another in a laundry basket by the foot of the stove. Mousers, probably. The farmers couldn't afford to carry passengers, and she guessed even the cats had to earn their keep.

Anne tipped out a pile of dough onto the worktop and kneaded it vigorously till the kettle boiled, then dropped it back into the bowl and stood it on the back of the range beside the cat and the washing to prove.

She made the tea—builders' tea, Rob would have called it. Laurie didn't call it anything. She just suppressed a shudder and asked for a little more milk.

Anne pushed the mug towards her and sat down opposite, regarding her assessingly. 'So, you're here for a break, are you?' she asked.

'That's right,' Laurie replied, wondering why it suddenly felt like a job interview. 'I'm just renting it for a while.'

Anne nodded, then went on candidly, with no attempt at subtlety or social pleasantries, 'Iain thinks you've run away from your husband—he said the fellow here at the weekend was very likely your fancy man. Well, that's your business, of course. I was just going to give you a word of advice—we don't care what folk get up to, but there's some about here take offence. You might want to be careful how you go on.'

Laurie stifled an astonished smile. 'I'm sorry to disappoint you, but he is my husband,' she said, 'and I haven't left him. I'm just sorting out my life. I wanted a little peace and quiet. I've got a business—it's a bit demanding, and Rob's always working, often away—we hardly ever see each other. I just wanted time to think—reassess.'

Anne snorted. 'Sounds like you've got plenty of that. I know how it is. The lambing season starts soon, and I don't see Iain from one day to the next, only to change his clothes and have a quick wash and a bite to eat. Sometimes there isn't even time for that. It goes on for weeks, and even when I do see him he's too tired to do anything but sleep. Then there's the grouse—he works as a gilly for one of the big estates, and from the twelfth onwards I don't see him for weeks again.'

'The twelfth?' she said, aware that she was missing something here.

Anne looked at her as if she was a bit dim. 'The twelfth of August,' she said patiently. 'The first day of the grouse shooting season. They spend all year looking after them, then go and shoot them. It's a business, just like yours, I guess, only probably bloodier.' She shrugged. 'You're not alone in finding your husband missing most of the time. I think that's just the way it is. No time for the important things. You just have to get on with it—and round here there's always plenty to do so I don't have time to get bored. As my grandmother would say, the devil makes work for idle hands.'

'I didn't have anything to do,' Laurie told her. 'That was the trouble. I was just at home being decorative. It wasn't enough—that's why I started my business.'

Anne looked at her searchingly. 'No children yet, then?' she said, and Laurie thought of the struggle they'd had, the heartache, month after month, the unspoken recriminations, the disappointment, and looked away.

'No,' she said lightly. 'Not yet.'

A floury, work-roughened hand covered hers. 'They'll come, lass,' Anne told her gently. 'Don't you fret. When the time's right, they'll come.'

And what if it's never right? Laurie thought sadly. What if it never is? What if I lose him?

'I expect you're right.' She made a performance of

looking at her watch. 'Heavens, is that the time? I must go,' she said abruptly. 'I've just remembered I've got to make an important call to someone before they go into a meeting. Thank you so much for the tea, though. It was lovely to meet you.'

She drank a little more of it, forcing it down, and stood up quickly. 'Don't move, I'll see myself out. Thanks again for all your help.'

'Any time. You take care, now, and call if you need anything.'

'I will.' She flashed a genuine smile of thanks, and let herself out, heading back down the track to her cottage. She felt a little guilty for bolting out so fast, but she really, *really* didn't want to get into the baby question with a stranger and Anne McGregor didn't seem reluctant to involve herself in other people's affairs. However kindhearted she might be, Laurie didn't need that.

She paused at the gate and looked around. It was a better day today, much milder, and the rain that had started last week had finally stopped, thank goodness. Not before the damage had been done, though.

She'd decided that Little Gluich meant small, sticky place. The run-off from the snow and rain all seemed to have pooled at the end of her garden, forming a bog, and she was glad the track was mainly stone or she didn't think she'd get the car out.

The dogs, on the other hand, seemed to love playing in the mud, and two muddy dogs in the house were a nightmare. Still, grooming them and running her business gave her something to do to occupy her time. She certainly wasn't short of activities—and fitting Anne

McGregor into the timetable had been a two-edged sword.

She thought of the woman's philosophical attitude and wondered if she could be so stoic. Probably not. She wanted a marriage—a partnership—and that meant a husband around to talk to and share things with, not what amounted to an absentee landlord.

Still, there hadn't been much of the absentee landlord about him the last couple of weekends. Her cheeks heated at the memory, and she wished she could have found the time to go down to see him this week. The trouble was, he wasn't in London anyway, he was in New York now from today, and probably wouldn't get back for this weekend either.

Hopeless. She'd just have to get on with the life she'd thought she wanted, but she wasn't so sure any more that she did. What she wanted was her old life back, not the one she'd just left, but the one where she worked with him, sharing decisions, getting involved, but it wasn't possible because his life had changed in the last couple of years.

He'd expanded his theatre of operations, started working much more abroad, and she'd been in limbo.

She sighed. He couldn't turn the clock back, and she couldn't expect him to, but there just didn't seem to be a place for her in his life now that was where she wanted to be.

She realised suddenly that far from her leaving him, he had actually left her, in many ways. She'd just been the one to make the geographical break by moving out. She'd lost him, and it looked as if the only way she could get him back was to stay here and make him come to her for the weekends.

'Fine,' she said out loud. 'So I'll ring him and invite him for the weekend.'

She went back into the cottage, endured the rapturous greeting from the dogs and rang the New York office. No reply, of course, because it was still only something before six in the morning and there would be no one in.

She went to work, but it didn't seem to hold her mind this morning. Only his website for the new company interested her, and she worked on it for the rest of the day, neglecting some of her other clients, and then guilt caught up with her and she ended up working on their jobs that night.

She tried Rob on and off during the day, but he wasn't in the New York office and they didn't seem to be expecting him. His mobile was switched off, too, which puzzled her. She left a message, but he didn't come back to her, so she just worked on to drown her foolish disappointment.

It was almost midnight when she saw lights coming down the track. Very late for a visitor, she thought, and stayed upstairs in the safety of the office to see who it was. Not that it was particularly safe up there if she had a determined intruder, but the dogs were barking furiously and that might be a bit of a deterrent.

She couldn't see much in the light from the lantern on the side of the garage. It was a small car, indeterminate, and it was only when the driver opened the door and the interior light came on that she realised it was Rob. Her heart skittered with joy, and abandoning her computer she ran down the stairs, opened the door and followed the dogs across the gravel.

She made herself go slowly instead of throwing herself across the drive into his arms like the dogs had done.

Not that he would have noticed. He had his hands full dealing with them.

Finally he pushed them down and straightened, and his smile made her heart flip over. 'Hi there. I thought I'd better come and check out this website.'

That wasn't what his smile said, though, and she went into his arms and kissed him lingeringly. 'I think that's a fine idea,' she told him with a smile, and led him into the cottage. 'Coffee?'

'Any of that malt whisky left?'

'Yes.'

'Both would be nice. And I really do want to see the website. Have you had time to do anything with my suggestions?'

'No, but I've done it,' she told him frankly. 'I expect I'll get an earful from some of my other clients, but never mind.'

He grinned. 'You're a star.'

She made him coffee and gave him a glass for the malt, and then they went over to the office and she showed him what she'd done, and all the time she was conscious of his body behind her, leaning over her to see the screen.

She could feel the warmth coming off his body, smell the enticing scent of his aftershave and the other, more subtle scents that were his alone, and she found her concentration wavering. Rob, though, was razor sharp as ever.

'I like that,' he said finally. 'Let's go for it.'

Absurd how those few words could warm her so much. She spun the chair round and smiled up at him. 'Thanks.'

'My pleasure.' He hesitated, then held out his hand. 'Time for bed?' he suggested, and her smile softened.

'That sounds like the best idea you've had for ages.'

'So glad you approve.'

It was like the weekend before last all over again. They finally fell asleep a little after three, and at six he woke, stretched and kissed her.

'I have to go,' he said, his voice gruff with sleep.

'So soon?' she said. She could feel a wave of disappointment swamping her. Surely he could stay a few more hours—

'I'm sorry. I stalled New York for a day—I had a few things I had to do in London, and by the time I'd finished it wasn't worth going over there. I thought I'd rather spend the night with you and travel on in the morning.'

'Are you flying from Glasgow?' she asked, and he nodded.

'Yes. Come downstairs with me. I need a coffee to kickstart me before I set off.'

She made the coffee while he showered, and they sat at the kitchen table, him in his suit, her in her nightshirt and dressing gown, and sipped coffee while she wondered how long they could live this way. It was crazy—even more crazy than before, and putting more pressure on him. She felt guilty, but then she told herself it was his choice. He wouldn't do it if he didn't want to, and at least he was noticing her now. That much was an improvement.

'I had dinner with Andy the other night,' he said suddenly.

She scanned his face warily. 'Really? Was Jonathan there?'

He shook his head. 'No. It was just us. She said there

would be others, but apparently they cancelled at the last minute and she didn't tell me Jonathan was away. She's a bit of a barracuda really, isn't she?'

'She's silly. She's got a good husband.'

'She said he's always away.'

She met Rob's eyes. 'He is—and she's bored. He shouldn't leave her alone so much.'

Something flickered in his eyes and was gone. 'She needs something to do. You were alone. You didn't start stealing other women's husbands.'

'No, but I've got a brain,' she pointed out. 'I don't think Andy has—or if she does, she doesn't want to bother to use it.' She searched his face. 'Did she come on to you?'

He grimaced. 'Yes, she did. Not massively. I told her I didn't play games. I also told her she needed to find something to do, and I told her about you. She was stunned. She thought you'd withdrawn from circulation because you were suffering from depression—you've obviously told her about the baby thing.'

Laurie pictured Rob alone with Andy, first being propositioned, then having his most private laundry aired in public, and she wanted to kill her friend—slowly and painfully. 'I mentioned it,' she said. 'She was telling me how lucky I was, and I was sick of hearing it. She caught me on a bad day. Did she give you the IVF lecture?'

He smiled a little grimly. 'She tried. I told her I felt it was jumping the gun a little.'

She nodded. It was irrelevant now, anyway. They had much more important things to worry about than the fact that she couldn't conceive.

He drained his coffee and set the mug down. 'I need to go. The flight won't wait for me. I'm going to have to buy my own plane if this goes on.' His grin was a little cockeyed, and she stood up and hugged him.

'I'm sorry,' she said into his shirt front, but he hugged her back and dropped a kiss on her head.

'Don't be sorry. It's just the way things are now. You go back to bed, I'll see you when I can get away. Maybe in about ten days.'

'OK.' She lifted her face for a kiss, and his mouth met hers and lingered. Finally he straightened and sighed.

'I'll see you. Take care—and thanks for doing the website. It's really good. You're a clever girl.'

He left her, warmed by his words, and the little glow of pleasure stayed with her all the way upstairs and into the bed. Then the scent of his body enveloped her, and she turned her face into the pillow and cried because he'd gone again and she didn't want him to.

'You're being silly,' she told herself, banging the pillow with her fist and rearranging it. 'Just stop it.'

But she couldn't, and she cried herself back to sleep.

He took five suits into the office and gave them to Sue on the following Monday. 'I don't suppose you could get these cleaned for me, could you?' he asked with an apologetic smile. 'And I could do with some new shirts. I seem to have mangled the others in the washing machine.'

'What size?' she asked, and jotted it down. 'Silk? Cotton?'

'Some of each. White. I don't like coloured shirts for work.'

She stifled the smile like a trooper and he felt a little guilty. How long had she known him? And he'd never worn a coloured shirt to work in all that time. 'Thanks,' he said, his answering smile wry, and she patted his shoulder.

'Don't worry about it. I'll do this, you look through that teetering pile on your desk. I can't seem to keep up with it, and if you want my opinion, which you probably don't, I don't think you're spending enough time in this office. You're spreading yourself too thin, Rob, and you look like hell.'

She went out, the door clicking shut behind her like a punctuation point, and he walked slowly over to his chair behind the desk and settled into it, staring blindly at the pile of paperwork that was waiting for him.

'Oh, Laurie,' he said softly. 'What's happening? When did everything go wrong?' He closed his eyes and rested his head on his hands, propping his elbows on the edge of the desk—the only empty part of it. He was exhausted. He'd been in New York until late on Friday, flown home and spent a few hours in bed before dragging everyone in the new company away from their families for an impromptu meeting yesterday.

And now he had Sue telling him off for not being here and not dealing with his workload. When, exactly?

He stood up and went to the window, staring down over the bustle and confusion that was London's rush hour. The only things that were moving were the pedestrians, hurrying about their business. The traffic was gridlocked as usual, and he had a sudden image of Little Gluich, like an oasis of calm in the frantic desert of his life.

He wished he'd had time to get up there, but there was no time. He couldn't see that he'd have time this coming weekend, either—not with Sue on the warpath about his dereliction of duty and Mike hopping from foot to foot needing decisions.

Sue came back in, her knock perfunctory. 'You look awful,' she told him bluntly. 'I'll get you a glass of iced water.'

'I want coffee.'

'Tough. You're having water.'

She walked out again and he sighed and scrubbed a hand through his hair. She was turning into a witch.

'Here. Drink this. When did you last have anything that wasn't based on caffeine or alcohol?'

He shrugged. He couldn't remember.

'I cleaned my teeth in water this morning,' he offered weakly, but she just gave him a withering look.

'You need to take better care of yourself if you're going to indulge in this punishing schedule—although, of course, if you're trying to win Laurie back then looking that rough could have its upside. At least this way she'll feel sorry for you.'

His mouth opened then closed again, snapping shut into a grim line.

'And don't give me a lecture about exceeding my authority,' she continued, levelling a finger at him. 'I've worked for you for six years—longer than you've known your wife. I'm not surprised she's gone, frankly. There's precious little to keep her here—and if you want her back, you're going to have to make some pretty radical changes.'

And with that she turned on her heel and stalked out, leaving him standing there motionless in the ringing silence like a cardboard cut-out. He wished he was. Cardboard cut-outs didn't have to make radical changes. They just stood there and let it all happen.

Which, when he thought about it, was rather what he was doing. Letting it all happen. If an opportunity came along, he took it, without thought or hesitation. He didn't have to do that. The company was big enough—more than big enough. He had more money than he knew what to do with, and no time to spend it except on more work, more investments, more companies that needed his attention.

He wanted to be back at Little Gluich, but it wasn't going to happen and he couldn't see a way round it.

He turned back to the window, staring blindly out over the heaving city. It was like an enormous ants's nest, writhing with life, and suddenly he hated it. He'd always loved it, thrived on it, but Laurie had shown him a little piece of heaven, and suddenly he could see the dross and chaos for what it was.

The buildings went out of focus, and he swallowed hard and blinked. Damn.

The door opened. 'You need to look at that paperwork, Rob,' Sue said crisply. 'It won't do itself.'

He dragged in a steadying breath and turned round. 'Get your pad. We'll do a bit of work, then I've got some calls to make.'

'You certainly have. Mike wants to speak to you—he says it doesn't matter what time, as soon as you can. He's in Paris, you can get him on his mobile. And you have to phone David Wright about the new website. They like it, but there's a problem. They don't feel it fits their image.'

'No—their perceived image doesn't fit the website,' he corrected, and Sue arched a brow.

'I'll let you tell him that. He's steaming—says you should have consulted with him on it.' She rattled off a list of other calls, and he sat down, suddenly overwhelmed. How long had it been like this? It was crazy. None of them could work at this pace.

'Are you happy?' he asked, cutting her off in midstream.

She looked at him in astonishment. 'Happy?' she said. She sounded stunned. 'No, not especially.'

'So why do you stay?'

She sat down on the chair opposite and met his eyes frankly. 'I don't know. For you? For Laurie? Because if I wasn't here you wouldn't have *any* time to spend with her?'

'What about your own social life?' he asked, suddenly realising just how little he really knew about her.

'We don't really have one. Because Joel's at home all day it's less of a problem than it might be. He looks after the children in the holidays, we go out occasionally at the weekends. We're just a normal family.'

'Does he think you work too hard?'

She laughed without humour. 'Just a bit. It's the only thing we row about.'

He shook his head. 'I'm sorry. You should have said something. Do you need an assistant?'

'I have an assistant,' she reminded him. 'Lucy. Remember?'

He did remember, vaguely. He seemed to be dealing with so many secretaries in so many places. It was only Sue that he'd really connected with, and it seemed he hardly knew anything about her. He didn't know the sex or age or names of her children, or how many she had, or what their problems had been—nothing.

He felt suddenly ashamed. 'I'm sorry,' he said gruffly. 'I seem to have lost touch with everything.'

She put her pad and pencil down and sat back. 'So what are you going to do about it, Rob? You can't go on like this, and neither can I, not really, and your wife's voted with her feet.'

He swallowed hard and looked away. He didn't need Sue, no matter how well-intentioned, seeing into the depths of his soul. He didn't even want to go there himself. 'Got any ideas?' he asked, and his voice sounded rusty and unused.

'Hand New York over to Mike. He's big enough to make his own decisions, but you tie him hand and foot and won't let him do it on his own. It drives him crazy. And stop buying companies just because you like the look of them. Turn them around if you must, but then sell them and let go of them. Forget Paris. It's nothing. It brings in a marginal amount of money compared to what you've got invested in it, and you don't need it. It's just another millstone, and Mike hasn't got time for it either.'

He looked up at her slowly, his eyebrow quirking. 'Is that all?'

She smiled a little awkwardly. 'It'll do for a start—and you did ask.'

'And what about Laurie?' he added softly. 'Got any ideas for what I can do about her?'

'Get your house in order first. Laurie'll keep. Then go and see her. Tell her what you've done. Ask her to come back.'

'I don't know if she will.'

'Well, she won't yet, that's for sure. You need to get radical, Rob. Get to it.'

He nodded slowly. 'OK. Get me Mike.'

She smiled and unfolded her legs and stood up, and

he looked at her and realised for the first time that she was a very lovely woman.

'Sue?'

She turned at the door.

'Thanks.'

'My pleasure.'

'I don't suppose,' he said, pushing his luck, 'there's any coffee on the go?'

'I'll get you Mike while it brews.'

He smiled, and with a cheeky wink she went out and shut the door.

He rubbed his hands together. They were sweating, and his heart was pounding. Adrenaline. Fight or flight.

And he was getting ready for the fight of his life.

Laurie was miserable. The weather was cold and wet and wretched, she was lonely, and her business didn't hold her interest any more. Been there, done that, she thought.

The phone rang, and it was Andy.

'Hello, stranger,' her old friend said brightly. Too brightly.

'Hi,' Laurie replied, a little wary. 'How are you? I gather from Rob that Jonathan's been away.'

'Oh, isn't he always? Not as away as you, though. You might have said something.'

'I'm sorry. It was a last-minute thing,' she said, not bothering to add that Andy would have been the last person she'd tell, close as they'd been. The town crier had nothing on her.

'So when are you coming back?' Andy asked, and Laurie hesitated.

'I'm not sure. Why?'

She could almost hear the shrug. 'Just curious. It seems a little dangerous to leave that man alone down here while you go off to your Scottish retreat.'

'He comes to stay,' she said, posting hands-off signals all over him, but it was too subtle for Andy. Either that or she had her own agenda, which was more likely.

'It's a long way to go for sex,' she said, and Laurie thought she could detect a thread of warning in her friend's voice. 'Especially when there's plenty available much nearer home.'

Laurie stared at the receiver in astonishment. 'Are you trying to tell me something?' she said bluntly.

'Just a friendly warning. He's too good a catch to leave unattended. It's not just me, darling, there are hundreds of women out there who'd kill to be in your shoes, but I have to say if you're leaving him for keeps, I'd appreciate a tip-off.'

'Andy, you're married!' she said, scandalised. 'What about Jonathan?'

'What about him? He's been impotent for three years, Laurie. That's why we haven't got kids. Trust me, Rob's a much better bet.'

Impotent? Poor Jonathan. She dragged her mind back to what Andy was saying. 'Rob's never at home either.'

'Perhaps that's because it's not welcoming enough,' she said.

There was a soft click, and the dialling tone sounded in Laurie's ear. She put the phone down and stared blindly out of the window. Was Andy really threatening her, or was she just trying to bring her to her senses?

Lord knows, but it gave her something to think about.

She switched off her computer, got up and went out

with the dogs for a long, thoughtful walk. At the end of it they were all muddy and tired, but at least she now knew what she was doing.

She just hoped Rob would agree.

CHAPTER TEN

ROB worked flat out for the next four days, rescheduling his life, off-loading work, companies—all manner of things. He changed his car, too. A saloon was no good for what he had in mind.

Sue said nothing. She just worked tirelessly beside him, helping him with the administrative details of his radical shake-up. The only hint she gave that she was pleased was an occasional approving smile. Nothing more, but it kept him on track, and gave him hope. If Sue thought he was doing the right thing, then with any luck Laurie would, too.

Please, God.

Early on the Friday morning he set off in his brand new Mercedes estate and drove to Scotland, arriving unannounced at the cottage in mid-evening.

He hadn't phoned to warn her because he'd wanted to take her by surprise. He liked doing that. She always seemed pleased to see him. That probably ought to give him confidence, he thought, getting out of the car, but somehow it didn't.

Not enough.

His heart was banging against his ribs, his blood pressure must be sky high, and he realised that the next few minutes were probably going to be the most important of his life. That was pretty scary. Drawing in a deep breath, he raised his hand to knock on the door just as she opened it.

'Rob.'

No rapturous welcome—at least, not from her. The dogs were doing their usual ecstatic thing, but she was thoughtful and silent. He pushed them down and straightened, searching her unsmiling face for clues.

'Are you OK?' he asked, and she smiled then, a little, strained smile that didn't really reach her eyes.

'Yes. Of course. I just wasn't expecting you.'

She's got a lover, he thought with absolute and horrendous certainty. Oh, hell, she's got a lover, either here now or due here shortly.

'Is it inconvenient?' he asked, his heart in suspense, but she shook her head and opened the door wider.

'Of course not. It's just—well, like I said, I wasn't expecting you.' She rubbed her hands together nervously. At least, he assumed it was nerves. He'd never seen her do it before. 'I was coming to see you, actually,' she said, lifting her chin. 'I've got something to say to you.'

She looked so serious that his heart, on the point of overdrive, beat even harder. She was going to ask for a divorce, he thought. Oh, no. Please, no, not that.

'I've got something to say to you, too,' he said tautly. 'That's why I'm here. So, who's going first?'

'Why don't you?' she said, turning away so he couldn't see her eyes. 'I'll make some coffee.'

He hadn't had any for days, on Sue's instructions, but he wasn't going to say no. Not now. He would have asked for some of the malt whisky, but he was probably about to have to start driving again, judging by the drawn look on her face and her huge and smudgy eyes with their unreadable expression.

He followed her into the kitchen and sat down at the

table she'd threatened to burn when they were snowed in. It looked curiously tidy in there. She must have had a blitz. For the boyfriend? Oh, hell. He couldn't stand this.

'I've given New York to Mike,' he said abruptly, piling in without preamble or explanation. 'I've sold the Paris operation to someone who's been after it for months, I've advertised for an assistant and I've arranged to cut down on my travelling.'

She went absolutely still. 'Why the estate car?' she said in a strange voice.

He took a deep breath. 'For the dogs,' he said, and left it hanging there for her to work out.

She sat down opposite him slowly, and he thought if he touched her, she'd shatter. Her eyes were huge. 'I don't understand.'

He closed his eyes and counted to ten, then opened them and looked at her, letting her see right down inside him to the vulnerable and needy man who was so afraid of losing her. 'I love you, Laurie,' he said quietly. 'I can't go on like this. I need you in my life—properly in my life, not tucked away in some fantasy world where I can only come and see you from time to time, but with me in my bed every night, beside me, working with me, part of my life.'

He dragged in a shaky breath and went on, 'And if I can't have that, then—I guess it's goodbye.'

His voice faltered on the last word, and he dropped his eyes, unable to let her see inside him any more. Some things were just too close to home, too painful, too revealing—

'Rob?'

Her voice was gentle, but he could hardly hear it for the rushing in his ears and the agony of suspense.

'Rob, look at me.'

He lifted his head, using up the last of his courage, and saw she was smiling, her eyes shimmering with tears.

'I love you,' she said unsteadily. 'I was coming home. I'm all packed, the car's loaded, I was leaving in the morning. I didn't know if you'd want to see me, or if you'd want me back, but I need you, and if all I can have is the little bit of time you have left over after work, well, it'll have to be enough, because I can't live without you. You're all that matters to me, Rob, everything I care about, and I need to be with you.'

He stared at her speechlessly for an age, then somehow they were in each other's arms and he was holding her, wrapping her tight against his chest, and she was clinging to him as if she could never let him go. 'Thank God for that,' he said unevenly, 'because I need you, too, more than you'll ever know.'

'I think I can imagine,' she said with a shaky little laugh. 'Oh, Rob. Oh, thank God. I was so scared.'

He buried his face in her hair, pressing his lips to it. 'So was I—scared you'd say no, scared I'd left it too late, scared I'd lose you. Scared of everything. I don't know what I would have done if you'd told me you couldn't come back.'

She looked up at him, her eyes soft and swimming with tears of joy. 'Not a chance,' she said softly. 'I'm coming back, Rob, be sure of that. I'm coming back and I'm never leaving you again, not as long as I can breathe.'

His arms tightened convulsively around her, and he

dropped his head onto her shoulder and gave a ragged sigh. They stood there like that for ages, and then he lifted his head and looked down at her.

'Let's go to bed. I need to hold you, and I'm so tired I'm almost asleep on my feet.'

'What about the coffee?'

'What about the coffee? I don't want it, I want you. Nothing else. Just you.'

Nothing else. Just her.

That sounded good. They went to bed, taking turns in the bathroom on the way, and despite his exhaustion he still made love to her, slowly and tenderly, until she fell apart in his arms.

They slept till dawn, their bodies tangled together, and then made love again. Afterwards she lay sprawled half over him, her head pillowed on his chest, and thought that nothing could make her happier.

Well, that wasn't quite true, but she was as close as she was going to get.

Sadly she traced a little whorl of hair on his chest with her fingertip. 'Rob?'

'Mmm?'

'I'm so, so sorry I can't give you a baby,' she said quietly.

He was motionless for a fraction of a second, then his arms tightened and he cradled her closer against his chest, one hand soothing rhythmically against her spine.

'Don't be. It doesn't matter. I don't care any more. I don't know if I ever did, except for you. I don't need a baby. I just need you.'

'I'll have tests, if you want.'

He shook his head. 'Only if you want. Like I said, I

don't care. It's not what matters. I know that now. We'll do whatever you want—whatever you need.'

He kissed her gently, and she curled into his arms and let him hold her. It felt so good.

She wondered if they'd ever have a child. It would have been nice, but as he said, it didn't matter. Nearly losing him had shown her that, and she was glad in a way that they'd gone through the heart searching and agony of the past few weeks. It would make their marriage stronger as a result, she was sure, and that could only be a good thing.

'We ought to get up,' she said eventually. 'The poor dogs need their breakfast and a walk, and we've got a long way to go.'

'We don't have to hurry,' he told her. 'We can do it in two days.'

'What about the dogs?'

'We'll find a little hotel that takes dogs—a guest house or something.'

'Or we could just get up and go,' she suggested hopefully. 'My car's packed, all I have to do is strip the bed, pack my wash things and the last bits in the kitchen, put the dogs in the car and leave.'

He looked up at her. 'Do you really want that car?'

She stared back at him in surprise. 'Well—no, not really, I don't suppose, unless you've sold mine.'

He shook his head. 'No, of course not. And your BMW's an estate, so it'll do for the dogs. I just thought, if you don't want the Ford, we could sell it to a garage up here to save you having to drive all the way back. If everything goes in your car, it'll certainly go in mine, and if we share the driving we can do it easily in one day.'

'It would be nice to get home,' she said, thinking of her garden and how all the plants must be coming up. It was March now, and spring would have sprung, or started to, at least. She wondered what Minstrel would make of it, and thought she'd probably love it. She'd be in the little lake with Midas in no time flat.

'And what about this place?' Rob asked. 'Do you mind leaving it?'

She shrugged. 'Not really. It's been lovely, the time we've had together here, but it isn't really real, is it?'

She could feel his smile against her temple. 'Not really, no.'

'Anyway, it's only rented and they might not want to sell it. Why don't we just drop the key into the agent on the way through Inverness and settle up the bill?'

'Good idea,' he murmured, and gave her a quick squeeze. 'Last one in the bathroom's a sissy,' he said, and flicked back the quilt.

She laughed. 'You go. I'll strip the bed. If we go in there together we'll just get distracted.'

He grinned. 'You read my mind, you hussy.'

She swatted at him with one of the pillowcases. 'Go on, hurry up. I want to go home.'

It was a long day. By the time they turned onto the lane that led to their house, she was wilting. She'd driven for a little way in the middle of the day, but only long enough for Rob to have a quick snooze beside her, and then he'd woken up again, stretched and yawned and thrown her a grin, and she'd pulled over at the next services for a late lunch and they'd swapped again.

Now, though, she was wide awake. It was dark as they turned onto the drive, but the lights came on automatically as they drove up and she could see the daffodils lining the drive, their pale gold heads nodding a welcome as they passed.

Things were greening up; the shrubs were in bud, and everything in the garden was way ahead of Scotland, as she'd known it would be. When Rob drew the car to a halt and she opened the door to get out, she could feel why instantly. It was warmer, much warmer, mild and welcoming, and she could smell new-mown grass in the night air.

She could hear traffic in the distance, extraordinarily intrusive after the silence of Scotland, and yet somehow comforting. Home, she thought, breathing in the mild air and sighing with relief.

She wasn't the only one who was relieved. Rob had opened the tailgate, and the dogs were running round, noses down, and Midas looked ecstatic. He rushed from place to place, Minstrel in hot pursuit, sniffing every blade of grass, every shrub, everything in the wide sweep of the front garden while Rob stood there with his arm round her and they watched them contentedly. Finally they came back to her call, tongues lolling, and looked expectantly from Rob to Laurie.

'I think they'd like supper,' Laurie said with a smile.

'What about you? Want me to get something in for us?'

She shook her head. 'No. I just want a nice cup of tea and time to get settled in again. It feels so odd to be home, and yet so good.'

She turned to him and reached up, drawing him down and kissing him lingeringly. 'Thank you for coming to get me. I was so afraid you wouldn't want me back.'

'Why would I not want you back?' he asked with a

wry smile. 'It was me that was the idiot.' His voice was light, but she could see the sincerity in his eyes.

'We won't argue about it,' she said. 'Dogs, come on, let's go inside.'

It seemed oddly unfamiliar. Huge, for a start. The hall was vast and echoing, the kitchen a cavern, the drawing room and dining room seemed far too big and grand for normal functioning. The morning room was a little formal, the study too masculine.

The breakfast room was the only room she felt right in, and she headed for it, Rob and the dogs in train.

'This is a lovely room,' she told him. 'We don't use it nearly enough. We ought to have a sofa in here for the dogs and us to curl up on.'

He raised a brow and laughed softly. 'Just one sofa? For all of us?'

She shrugged and grinned. 'It would be cosy. You could keep me company while I cook.'

'Do what you like. Whatever makes you happy—whatever will make you stay.'

There was a trace of vulnerability in his voice, and she put her arms round him and hugged him again. 'I'm staying,' she told him firmly. 'Whatever happens in the future, I'm staying—unless you want me to go. Even then, I ought to warn you, I won't go without a fight.'

His arms tightened round her. 'Good. Now why don't you put your feet up and I'll feed the dogs and make you a cup of tea.'

'No sofa.'

'Go in the drawing room.'

She shook her head. 'I'm fine here.'

She sat down at the table, close enough to watch him as he pottered about the kitchen feeding the dogs, putting the kettle on, emptying the dishwasher. Homely, domestic things she'd hardly ever seen him do. She wondered how long it would last.

Weeks? Months? Years?

Maybe. He'd seemed sincere enough.

She felt exhausted. A sofa would be the first thing she'd buy, not new, but an old comfy second-hand one, already broken in and a bit down-at-heel so nobody had to feel precious about it.

'I'll get the stuff in from the car,' he said, but she shook her head.

'Not tonight,' she said, too tired to face the thought of all that unpacking. 'I only need that little bag I put in this morning. Everything else can keep—oh, except the two dog beds. We'll need them.'

He nodded and disappeared, coming back through the utility room laden with things. He must have put the car in the garage, she thought, her brain struggling to analyse everything and failing. Heavens, she was exhausted.

'Here you are, dogs. Where do you want to sleep?'

'Nowhere for a while,' she said with a laugh. 'Too busy sniffing round everything.'

Well, Midas was. Minstrel was like a shadow at his side, worried by the changes, her eyes sliding sideways to check on Laurie.

'It's all right, sweetheart,' she said softly. 'It's OK.'

The dogs came to her, leaning in stereo against her legs so she could stroke them.

'Time for bed,' Rob said a little later. The dogs had been out and were settling down at last, and she could hardly keep her eyes open another minute. Where he got his reserves from, she wasn't sure.

He picked up both bags in one hand and helped her to her feet with the other.

'Come on, upstairs. You look all in.'

He practically had to carry her. In the end he did, dropping the bags on the stairs and scooping her up into his arms.

'I can walk,' she told him, not at all sure it was true, but he carried her anyway and she was quite contented. It felt good. Right, somehow—like being carried over the threshold.

A new beginning.

He set her gently down on the bed and went back for the bags. 'You go first in the bathroom,' he said. 'I'll unpack your case.'

She nodded, took her washbag and nightshirt and wandered into the familiar-yet-unfamiliar en suite bathroom. Huge, again. Everything was huge. She washed quickly and went back to the bedroom, to find Rob putting the cases out onto the landing.

'Go on, into bed,' he said firmly, and a few moments later he joined her.

For the first time in ages, he didn't make love to her, just folded her close against his chest and sighed contentedly. 'It's so good to have you home,' he said quietly.

She wriggled closer. 'It's good to be home,' she told him. 'It feels odd—everything seems very big after Little Gluich, but I dare say I'll get used to it again.'

'Of course you will. And if you want to change anything, you know you can.'

'Not now,' she said drowsily. 'Now I just want to sleep...'

She drifted off, her voice fading, and as she slipped

over the edge into oblivion, she heard him murmur, 'I love you...'

It was wonderful to have her back. She'd been in his arms all night. He'd had cramp in his shoulder at one point, but he hadn't had the heart to move her, and after a while it had worn off. He'd have hellish pins and needles when she shifted her head, but it was worth it just to hold her. He'd had six long weeks without her, if he counted being away in New York before she'd gone to Scotland. Six weeks, with only the odd stolen weekend together to keep him sane.

Pins and needles seemed a small price to pay to have her back.

She moved, rolling away from him, flinging her arm out to the side. He eased his arm from beneath her and massaged it, wincing as the blood flow returned.

He slipped out of bed and pulled on his dressing gown. The sun was shining on the curtains, and he ran down and let the dogs out, put the kettle on and laid a tray. She'd need a cup of tea before she got up, he thought. Nice, slow start to the day—or maybe she'd have a lie-in.

He went back up and set the tray down on the bedside table, sat on the side of the bed and kissed her.

'Wake up, sleepy-head. Time for tea.'

She moaned and snuggled into his side, and he laughed and poured the tea, then went back round to his side of the bed with one of the mugs and got in beside her. 'Come on, Mrs Ferguson. You can manage to open your eyes.'

She rolled towards him, opened them a crack and then shut them again. 'Tired,' she mumbled, and so he drank his tea, then hers, and eventually left her there while he attended to the dogs. He fed them, then put them out again for a moment, then went back up.

She was sitting on the edge of the bed looking pasty, and he frowned.

'Are you all right?'

'I will be,' she said. 'I'm just so tired. I think it's all the emotion. I was so scared you wouldn't want me back.'

'Silly girl.' He sat beside her and hugged her. 'How about a nice soak in the jacuzzi?'

'Mmm.'

'Want company?'

She smiled wanly. 'I always want your company.'

He ran the water, then went to fetch her. 'Come on, your majesty. Your bath awaits,' he said with a grin, and she let him peel her out of her nightshirt and lead her to the bathroom.

It was one of those decadent tubs with two headrests, one at each end, so you lay head to toe and faced each other. He eyed her critically as she slid under the water. She seemed thinner, her ribs more prominent, making her breasts seem fuller somehow. She hadn't been feeding herself properly, he thought. No meat. Silly girl.

Well, if she wouldn't eat it, he'd have to find something else to tempt her with.

He turned the bubbles on, and she sighed contentedly and closed her eyes. 'That's gorgeous,' she said, and he smiled. She'd always liked it. Perhaps it would help to relax her.

She seemed a little tense about the house—not sure of it any more, as if she didn't feel at home here. That worried him, but not unduly. If it was only the house, he could deal with it. Change the colours, change the furniture, move walls—move house, if necessary. Nothing was impossible.

So long as she was happy with him…

She felt dreadful. Tired—so tired she could hardly drag herself around, and shaky. She'd been silly and spent too long in the jacuzzi, she thought. Too many bubbles, too much hot water.

She ate a slice of toast, but she only had fruit juice with it. Coffee had no appeal—not clean enough on the palate. Anyway, there wasn't really time to linger, because the dogs were looking hopeful, so Rob got her boots out of the car and they went for a walk, introducing Minstrel to the garden.

It was a glorious day, and she felt more at home outside, strolling down the paths and over the rolling lawns with Rob at her side and the dogs rushing hither and yon in search of new and more exciting smells.

Minstrel didn't go in the lake, and nor, with a little persuasion, did Midas. Good. She didn't feel up to bathing them both, and there was some gorgeous black mud near the edge on one side that he just loved to bounce around in.

'I think spring's coming,' Rob said, pointing out the buds on the trees. 'The willows are opening—there are catkins, look.'

There were, little yellow fluffy catkins like miniature bottlebrushes. She'd pick some for the house later, if she felt more energetic. The journey had taken it out of her—that and the strain of not knowing how he'd react.

'About your business,' he said carefully, and she turned her head so she could see his face.

'What about it?'

He shrugged. 'I just wondered if you wanted a proper office, or if you liked it at home, if you need to convert the rest of the attic and have some help—I want you to know you can do whatever you think best.'

She laughed wearily. 'I don't know what I think best. It seems awful, but I don't think I want to do it any more. It just doesn't interest me now—I've done it. I know I can. That's enough.'

'You could always come back to me, part-time, anyway. I know you won't want to be tied full-time because of the dogs, but if you want, I'd love to have you back. It doesn't seem the same without you.'

She swayed slightly and his arm tightened round her, hugging her closer to his side.

'Are you OK?'

'Mmm. Just tired. I felt a bit dizzy.'

He looked down at her, his eyes concerned, and suddenly they seemed to go out of focus and blur.

'Rob?' she murmured, puzzled, and then the light seemed to close in from the edges of her vision, until even the centre went black and she felt herself begin to fall…

He caught her, scooping her into his arms and cradling her against his chest. Heavens, she weighed nothing. He hadn't noticed last night, but today she seemed unbelievably light and fragile.

'Midas, Minstrel, come on,' he called, and hurried back up the lawn to the house. She was coming round, moaning softly, clinging to him.

'Rob?'

'Laurie? Are you OK?'

'What happened?'

'I don't know. You fainted.' He kicked his boots off and hooked the kitchen door shut behind him, leaving the muddy dogs in there, and took her through to the drawing room. Her own boots were wet and a little muddy, and he eased them off and then lifted her feet up onto the arm, raising them above her head.

'You stay there, I'm going to call the doctor.'

'I'm fine, Rob,' she protested weakly. 'I'm just tired. It was the hot bath—'

'I'm getting the doctor,' he repeated, scanning her pale face. She looked like death warmed up, and panic started to leak in round the edges of his self-control. She'll be fine, he told himself. She's just tired. She's right, it was the hot bath.

He didn't believe a word of it. He was suddenly, terribly afraid that there was something awful wrong with her, something incurable that would snatch her from him just as he'd got her back.

He dialled the surgery with trembling fingers and then waited anxiously with her until the doctor came. It wasn't their own doctor, but a duty doctor. Please God let him know what he was doing.

'Rob, I'm all right,' Laurie said again and again. All the time they were waiting she reassured him, but it was pointless. He could see her pallor, see the deep weariness inside her. Maybe this was why she'd never conceived—some terrible disease that only manifested itself when it was too late.

The big C?

Oh, lord, no. Not his Laurie.

The dogs barked, and he went to the front door just as a slim young woman emerged from her car. Well, maybe not so young, he thought, looking at her, but slender and elegant and with an air of confidence about her that made him relax a fraction.

'Dr Withers?' he said, just to check, although the big black bag should have given her away.

She smiled and held out her hand. 'Hi, there. You must be Mr Ferguson. Where's the patient?'

'In the drawing room, lying down. She looks awful.'

'OK. Let's go and have a look at her.'

She followed him into the drawing room, put her bag down on the floor by the settee and perched on the edge of it next to Laurie, taking her hand.

'Hi, Mrs Ferguson. I'm Maureen Withers. Your husband tells me you've fainted.'

She nodded. 'I'm just tired. It was a long day yesterday—we drove back from Scotland.'

'Lucky you. I love Scotland. Been on holiday?'

'No—well, I rented a cottage to get away from it all for a bit.'

'Mmm-hmm. On your own?'

'I've been up a few times to see her, in between work commitments,' Rob chipped in.

'Uh-huh. It's been a bit rough up there, I gather. Did you see any snow?'

Rob gave a grunt of laughter. 'Just a bit.'

'I expect it was very pretty. I love snow, but it's always so dirty round here.'

She was taking her pulse as they spoke, but she didn't seem to find anything untoward, because she stopped doing it without even consulting her watch. She rummaged in her bag and came out with a pen light, and shone it in Laurie's eyes in turn.

'Well, they're fine. Banged your head at all?'

'No.'

'Had breakfast?'

'A slice of toast.'

Rob snorted. 'She ate half of it and gave the rest to the dogs.'

Maureen Withers smiled. 'OK. How about periods? Are they regular?'

Laurie's mouth pulled into a slight grimace. 'As clockwork. We've been trying for ages to have a baby.'

'And when was your last period?'

Her eyes fell. 'I don't know the exact date—it was before I went to Scotland. Just before—it started on the Tuesday, and I went up on Thursday. It's why I went—I couldn't go through it all again.'

'And that was how long ago?'

'Five weeks,' Rob said, his voice sounding strange to his ears. 'All bar a couple of days. The lease on the cottage ran from the seventh of February. It's the tenth of March today.'

'So that's the fifth of Feb we're talking about—four weeks and five days?' Maureen said thoughtfully. 'OK. Any other symptoms apart from tiredness? Any breast tenderness or swelling? Peeing more often? Nausea? Off tea or coffee? Reacting to smells?'

Laurie swallowed. 'Well—a bit, perhaps.'

'Which?'

'Most of them, when I think about it,' she said slowly.

The doctor straightened up and smiled. 'Well, I think that's your answer. We'll do a test just to be on the safe side, but I don't think there's any doubt in my mind.'

Rob was stunned. 'You mean—?'

'I think your wife's probably perfectly well, Mr

Ferguson. I think you're going to have a baby. Let's just check.'

The next few minutes were agonising. Please, let it be, he thought. Please, because if it's a baby, it means it's nothing else, and I couldn't bear to lose her.

'Well, I think that's pretty conclusive,' Maureen Withers said, coming out of the cloakroom with a smile. 'Congratulations. You're going to have a baby—round about the twelfth of November, I reckon. I'll let your GP know. You'll need to go along for antenatal checks periodically, but just rest, eat plenty and time will cure your symptoms.'

Her smile swam out of focus. Rob closed his eyes and swallowed hard. When he opened them again Laurie was crying and laughing all at once, holding out her arms to him. He went into them, hugging her hard against his chest, fighting the urge to cry with her. She was all right. She was going to be all right. He wasn't going to lose her.

They heard the soft click of the door and looked up to find the doctor had gone.

'Are you OK?' she asked him, and he laughed a little shakily.

'I should be asking you that.'

She smiled, a deeply contented smile that he'd seen before on pregnant women but had feared he'd never see on Laurie.

'Oh, I'm fine. Never better. And at least we know now what's wrong with the house.'

'The house?'

'Mmm. I want to change things—I thought it was because I didn't like it any more, but it isn't. I'm just nesting.' She grinned at him. 'Don't worry, I'll be too tired to trash the place very much.'

Her grin changed, becoming more cheeky. 'I don't suppose you want to buy a company, do you? It's a very good one—they design websites. Only the designer's going to be taking maternity leave, apparently.'

'I wonder which company that could be,' he said drily, and smiled. It was hard not to. He had a lot to smile about. He tucked her under his arm, led her into the kitchen and sat her down. 'First things first. Just as soon as you're feeling well enough, we're going out to buy you a comfy old sofa.'

She sighed contentedly. 'Sounds good to me.'

The dogs looked from one to the other of them and whined, then went back to their beds and flopped down with a sigh.

'Happy?' he asked her, a little cautious, because she had said she wasn't sure she wanted a baby not so very long ago.

'Ecstatic,' she said softly. 'How about you?'

'So long as you are.'

'Oh, yes.'

'Then I'm happy,' he said, knowing it was true. 'I'm more than happy. I'm the luckiest man alive.'

She laughed. 'Just remember that when the baby's keeping you up all night,' she said, but he just smiled and hugged her again.

EPILOGUE

HE LAY in bed, listening in contentment to the soft sounds of the baby suckling at Laurie's breast.

She was quiet at last—she'd had colic a little while ago, her tiny legs drawn up while she screamed, and he'd walked her up and down for an hour before she'd settled—and by then, of course, she'd been starving hungry.

There was nothing he could do about that, so he'd handed her back to mum for a while and lay and watched them in the half-darkness. The baby's eyes were shut, her rosebud lips fastened greedily to Laurie's nipple, and Laurie was watching her as if she were the most precious thing in the world.

Finally the rhythmic sucking ceased, and Laurie turned her head and smiled at him.

'I don't suppose the luckiest man alive wants to do a nappy, does he?'

Rob chuckled. 'I expect he can manage it.'

He rolled over and swung his legs over the side of the bed, stretching gloriously before going round to take the baby from her mother.

'Hello again, my precious,' he said softly. 'Mummy tells me you need a new nappy. Can this be true? Again?'

She burped on his bare shoulder, and he closed his eyes with a chuckle and wiped up the little mouthful of warm milk with a tissue Laurie handed him.

'Still lucky?'

'Still lucky,' he said firmly, and went into the little nursery they'd made out of their dressing room. It only took moments to change the nappy, then he tucked her back into her cot on her side, covered her lightly with the blanket and stood looking down at her.

Their little miracle, he thought, although she probably wasn't a miracle. When he really considered it, it was no wonder Laurie hadn't conceived. They'd been so busy, he'd been away so much, the opportunities had hardly been there. That had changed. In the past year he'd hardly been away at all, and they were both much happier for it.

Laurie had attacked the house with enthusiasm, bringing warmth and light and colour into it, and the kitchen was now the hub of the house. He loved it, and so did she, and the dogs were more than happy to have their company.

He turned down the light, blew the baby a kiss and went back to Laurie.

'OK?' she asked softly.

'Fine. How about you?'

'The luckiest woman alive,' she said, snuggling contentedly up to his side.

He smiled in the darkness.

'The perfect couple, then. Just imagine that.'

'The perfect family,' she corrected.

'Almost.'

'Almost?' she said, stiffening, a note of concern in her voice.

'Mmm. We've got another one point four babies to work on yet.'

She relaxed again, her breath teasing his skin as she

laughed. 'Now there's a thought.' He felt her fingers walking on his chest, idly teasing, migrating south with casual purpose. 'I saw the doctor today.'

He lassooed her hand before it went any further. 'And?' he asked in a slightly strangled voice.

'And she gave me the all clear. Said everything was fine. So, if you're not too tired...'

There was a wail from the nursery, and Laurie rolled onto her back and laughed in despair. 'Still think you're the luckiest man alive?' she asked, and he nodded.

'Absolutely,' he replied. 'Oh, yes. Absolutely. Just do me a favour.'

'Yes?'

'Wait for me.'

'Forever,' she said, and he knew she meant it.

He bent and kissed her. 'I'll hold you to that,' he promised softly, and kissed her again.

And again.

And again...

WHITE
WEDDINGS

Beautifully romantic and traditional love stories don't get any better than those written by international bestselling author Betty Neels!

THE BEST *of*

BETTY NEELS

Four classic novels that bring to readers her famous warmth and tenderness—promising you hours of delightful romance reading!

NEVER WHILE THE GRASS GROWS

NO NEED TO SAY GOODBYE

THE COURSE OF TRUE LOVE

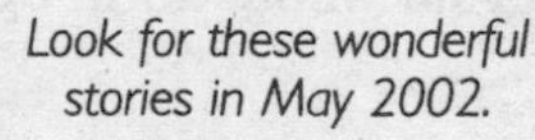

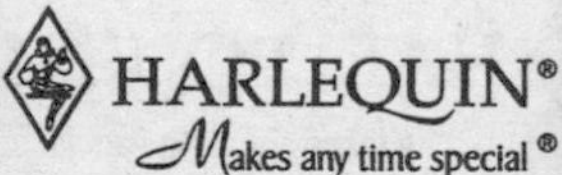

Visit us at www.eHarlequin.com

RCBN5